PRAISE FOR LAURIE FOO

"Foos's voice is a bold and tuneful guide in a world where nothing seems to fit."—*New York Times Book Review*

"Laurie Foos, like those maverick filmmakers the Coen brothers, follows her own quirky obsessions. . . . Foos is a precise writer who writes about messy things. She knows the stuff that ties women up, makes them slightly hysterical, and she stretches those fears to a surreal degree." —*Seattle Times*

"Foos takes off from Jeanette Winterson and goes for the baroque, surreal, and witty." —*Ms. Magazine*

"Foos's writing is always clear and clearly intelligent satire with its heart in the right place." —*Detroit Free Press*

"Foos will capture your heart, stroke your funny bone, and help you to see the depth of a woman's soul." —*Small Press*

"Foos is a writer who's going places." —*Entertainment Weekly*

Before Elvis

There Was Nothing

by Laurie Foos

COFFEE HOUSE PRESS

2005

Coffee House Press books are available to the trade through our primary distributor, Consortium Book Sales & Distribution, 1045 Westgate Drive, Saint Paul, MN 55114. For personal orders, catalogs, or other information, write to: Coffee House Press, 27 North Fourth Street, Suite 400, Minneapolis, MN 55401.

Coffee House Press is a nonprofit literary publishing house. Support from private foundations, corporate giving programs, government programs, and generous individuals help make the publication of our books possible. We gratefully acknowledge their support in detail in the back of this book. To you and our many readers across the country, we send our thanks for your continuing support.

LIBRARY OF CONGRESS CIP DATA
Foos, Laurie, 1966–
Before Elvis there was nothing : a novel / by Laurie Foos.
p. cm.
ISBN-13: 978-1-56689-168-4 (alk. paper)
ISBN-10: 1-56689-168-x (alk. paper)
1. Women—Fiction.
2. Presley, Elvis, 1935–1977—Influence—Fiction.
3. Abnormalities, Human—Fiction.
4. Missing persons—Fiction.
5. Agoraphobia—Fiction.
6. Horns—Fiction. I. Title.
PS3556.O564B44 2005
813'.54—DC22
2004028141

FIRST EDITION | FIRST PRINTING
1 3 5 7 9 8 6 4 2
Printed in Canada

For my aunt, June Fasso, whose courage inspires
and whose love for Elvis and family abides

Before Elvis
There Was Nothing

PART I

I always felt that someday,
somehow, something would happen
to change everything for me.

—ELVIS PRESLEY

ONE

You want to know about the horn. Of course you do. It's what everyone wants. To poke. Prod. Get inside. Understand.

I don't mind telling you about it—not anymore. In the beginning it was difficult, especially since it didn't become a horn for some time but started as a spot two inches above my eyebrow line. It was always perfectly centered; I parted my hair using it as a kind of compass. Why not find some practical uses? I am, after all, a hair replacement specialist, and we're nothing if not practical—that is, if you can put any stock in the benefits of hair addition or any of the other therapies we use once you've had a six-inch horn jutting from your forehead.

For a list of the different kinds of therapies available to women who have lost hair due to (a) chemotherapy; (b) alopecia; c) stress; (d) burns; or (e) plain bad luck, you can talk to me at the end of the story.

The horn is not me, and I am not the horn.

All right, then. Let's begin.

TWO

My parents left us for Elvis Presley. Or so my sister believes. But that's another story. I'll get to it in time.

I first noticed the horn—or at least, what were the beginnings of the horn—on my sister Lena's thirty-sixth birthday.

At first it was little more than a bump, a raised blemish, the kind of acne that plagues teenagers in the throes of a hormonal uproar, only this bump wasn't red and angry-looking but flesh-colored, as if someone had shoved a piece of styrofoam under my skin. Since I worked so much with styrofoam when I was studying to be a hair replacement specialist—don't call us beauticians or hairdressers; it's demeaning—combing out wigs and learning to weave strands of hair together, you could say I knew styrofoam intimately. In fact, that was just what I told Lena when I discovered the bump that day in the bathroom at her house.

She was getting ready for her birthday party, an event which always sparked her anxiety, especially since this particular year marked the eighteenth anniversary of our parents' departure. Eighteen years they'd stayed around, and eighteen years gone. Not only had the years doubled, she said, but also the pain. She began to panic as the minutes passed, unwrapping the paper plates and cups, glancing at the cake box in the refrigerator, and then running into the bathroom to splash cold water on her face and hyperventilate.

"Feel this," I said, trying to get her to focus on my forehead as her chest heaved with shallow breath. I held her index finger and moved it across the bump below my bangs. "Doesn't it feel just like styrofoam? I mean, I know a lot about styrofoam. You could even say I know it intimately."

But she was too preoccupied with her birthday and the desperate hope of finally receiving a card to think of anything else. No matter how many times I'd pleaded with her, every year she would leave two extra pieces of cake by the front door—just in case our parents showed up but decided not to join the party.

If they could leave us with hardly a word, then why the hell would they show up to watch her blow out the candles? I thought. *Let them buy their own goddamned cake in the shape of a hound dog,* but I could never say this to her.

"For God's sake, Cass," she said, "put some cream on it. Ernie hasn't brought the mail yet, and you know what that could mean."

Even though Lena had predicted our parents' departure years before they actually left, she was ever steadfast in her hope that they would come back.

Some people are like that about their parents. I'm not one of them.

She ran out of the bathroom before I could ask her what kind of cream she was talking about—exfoliating, moisturizing, or maybe even Retin-A. I rummaged in the medicine cabinet through all her bottles of pills and found some Noxzema. She had no use for beauty products, never even wore makeup, and since she never left the house, who could blame her? I remember wondering what possible effect Noxzema would have on styrofoam, if any. The skin wasn't dry or cracked, just raised about a quarter of an inch, enough to be aware of it, but no cause for alarm. At least not then.

To understand the horn, you have to understand our history.

You can make the obvious connections between the horn's eruption—if "eruption" is the right word—and our parents' disappearance, or between Elvis and the horn, or you may even think that the horn was a kind of belated birthday present to Lena, or that it was a manifestation of my own repressed hope that our parents would return.

But I'd say you should look elsewhere. Play armchair psychologist if you want, but I won't supply the armchair.

With two fingers I massaged the cream into the bump, lifting my bangs away from my forehead and rubbing in circles—not too much pressure, but enough for the cream to be absorbed. The bump was hard, but didn't show any sign of blisters or pus even as I squeezed it to see if it would burst. (I knew better than this, of course—you can try to extract a blemish, but I'm not big on extraction, even though one of the aestheticians at the spa where I work is what we call "extraction happy." We do what we can with skin and hair, but let's face it, we can't work miracles.) I could hear the echo of Lena's ragged breath as I closed the medicine cabinet and sprayed my hair flat against my forehead with some hair spray I found on her countertop. I could at least try to hide it. I didn't have any supplies with me, not so much as a tube of concealer. I was *that* unprepared.

When I found her, she was in the kitchen with a paper bag over her mouth and nose, waiting for me as she hyperventilated.

"Do you want me to get you a Xanax?" I asked, when I saw how quickly the bag was filling up and collapsing in on itself, faster than her usual attacks.

She shook her head and sucked at the bag.

"Ernie will be here soon," I said. "He must be on overtime today."

Since our parents' disappearance, I'd sent her mock birthday cards and had them mailed without postmarks. Ernie, the mailman, was invaluable in this regard. Of course Lena always realized minutes after opening them that the cards were fakes, but I liked to give her hope. You might say I conspired in her hopefulness.

When you're a sister, there's no telling what you'll do. I'd spent all day trying to think of something to wish her that year, some heartfelt hope of success sent to her by Ma and Our Father from wherever they might be, eating peanut butter and banana sandwiches and listening to Elvis. But everything I came up with sounded forced.

Dear Lena, I began, but every time I managed to scribble that phrase, the middle of my forehead would burn as if poked with a lit match. Our parents had disappeared one night when we were teenagers and had never been heard from again. They hadn't been kidnapped, and there had been no accidents, no last sightings at shopping centers or faces on milk cartons. Theirs had been a willful disappearance, and Lena and I—Lena more so than I—had come up with theories about where they might have gone. In recent years, it had become something of a game for me, and sometimes Lena joined in, but more often than not, talking about our parents—Ma and "Our Father," as we liked to call him—sent her into full-blown panic attacks.

Which was, of course, not a good thing.

We started calling him "Our Father" after he left. He was not a religious man but since he thought himself a disciple of the King, we decided to give him a name that smacked of the "King of Kings." Before they packed the car that night, Our Father had been a roadie for an Elvis impersonator named Rusty King for several years. Rusty was a natural redhead whose real name was Rusty Eastman, a name that Our Father felt was too close to that of Elvis's bodyguard, Red West, who had collaborated on the book that Our Father called "the one that killed Elvis." The details of Our Father's first meetings with Rusty were vague, but from what we'd been able to gather, Our Father had convinced him to become an Elvis impersonator one night after hearing Rusty sing, "Can't Help Falling in Love" in a parking lot outside a record store. After that night, Rusty bought himself a wig and a set of spangled jumpsuits and tried to work his way to Vegas. He played at local bars where Our Father sat in the wings, waiting to hand Rusty his scarves and glasses of water. Charlie Hodge, one of Elvis's Memphis Mafia guys, had done the same for Elvis, and Our Father was determined to give Rusty an air of authenticity.

Ma went to every show, but Lena and I were only invited once. We were about thirteen or fourteen at the time, but the bouncer let us in and fed us Cokes. Our Father waved to Ma from the wings and spilled water down the front of his black shirt. Lena and I giggled throughout the performance until we spotted Rusty teetering on the edge of the stage. We thought he was drunk, as Rusty so often was, but soon the place cleared and an ambulance arrived, taking Rusty off to a hospital and leaving all of their dreams of Vegas behind when Rusty was declared D.O.A.

"Another dead King," Our Father had said when he came home and sat at Ma's feet in the living room.

After the funeral, they never mentioned Rusty again, and Our Father gave up any hopes he'd had of ever making it to Vegas.

Lena and I were never particularly fond of Our Father when he was around, especially since he so rarely participated in our lives once he took up with Rusty. We loved Ma despite her shortcomings, but Our Father was often the butt of our jokes, to tell the truth. Once they were gone, though, our parents occupied Lena's thoughts nearly all the time. Lena's internet shrink had even said that she was developing an Electra complex. I had dreams about them nearly every night. In some of the dreams they played Twister with Elvis, their bodies contorted, Ma's toe over Elvis's right hand, Our Father's belt buckle pressed up against Ma's backside.

Elvis and Twister—and a few other things—were about all we had left of them, which, if you ask me, was more than enough.

For the past eighteen years Lena has spent much of her time hoping for word from Ma and Our Father, and in the process, she'd developed a friendship with Ernie that flourished after Boyd, her ex-husband, left her, and the agoraphobia kicked in. She'd met Ernie during her brief stint at the post office as a clerk, a job that ended once the panic attacks kept her indoors full time. Years later, there we were with Lena still sealed up in the house, living on the hope of a birthday card with no return address, and me with this bump on my head.

When her breathing slowed, Lena laid the paper bag on the table and lit a cigarette. Her hands shook, red blotches riding up her throat. I wanted to remind her that nicotine was a panic trigger, but she insisted that the nicotine's speeding of her pulse and heart rate served as a distraction. It comforted her, she said, to know her heart pounded for a specific reason and not simply because of her thoughts. She knew she could quit, she said, though she never chose to, and that made her feel powerful. I didn't understand the logic, but I was never one to argue with the things that could keep Lena calm. It was hard enough on her being in the house, and smoking gave her something to pass the time, she said. Besides Ernie and me and her internet shrink, the mail was one of Lena's only means of contact with the outside world. Her agoraphobia aside, I've often thought this was not necessarily a bad thing, especially since I spent so much time unable to go anywhere without being stared at, even before the horn's appearance.

"Appearance" may be a better word than "eruption." It's a word that Lena likes since she says it reminds her of Elvis and of me all at once. Both of us, she says, had much more inside than just the good looks that people liked to ogle.

As for the horn, I can only say that it took some time to appear and that it altered my appearance in ways I'd never have guessed.

Think of it as a slow burn, an expulsion of tissue from somewhere deep inside, someplace you never knew existed.

"If they do send a card this year," Lena said, exhaling a puff of smoke in my face, "then it will just prove what they knew all along, that I'd be right here in this house, alone."

I got up to get myself a glass of water. After Lena's attacks, I was always careful to measure my words.

"You'd be the one they'd contact, not me," I said, setting the glass on the table in case she wanted a sip. "One might say they always thought you were the most reliable."

I smiled to myself as I took several sips of water. I liked saying "one" instead of "you." Vance, the podiatrist I was seeing, always said "one."

"One should never cut one's toenails with a dull clipper," he'd say. "One should always use a pumice stone on the bottom of one's feet."

It gave him, I thought, a touch of class. At the very least, his education lent him an air of grace that none of my past boyfriends had. Most of them wanted me to lie naked beneath them while they expounded upon my beauty. On the street, I'd catch them stealing glances at other men as they passed by, their chests puffing up as the men's eyes followed me. Before Vance, I'd briefly dated a metrosexual who had his brows shaped and used up all my exfoliating creams. Vance paid little attention to my looks and even less to his own. His drooping ties and mismatched socks were actually endearing to me.

"I guess," Lena said, "but you never know."

I nodded.

"Exactly," I said. "One never knows."

I made tea and found a package of Lorna Doones while we waited for Lena's panic to subside. She had stacks of relaxation tapes and self-help books in every room of the house, though none of these had helped. Neither had wearing a rubber band on her wrist to snap herself when she felt unsteady, or breathing from her diaphragm and repeating the word "one" like a mantra. She'd had to modify the mantra from the original "ohmmmm" and "ahhhh," since it made her weep uncontrollably, sounding far too much like "Oh, Ma." She belonged to several telephone support groups and talked to her internet shrink three times a week, their instant messaging sometimes going on for hours. The best thing to do for her in these situations was to keep talking even when she fell silent, which normally didn't present a problem for me.

When it came to our parents, however, I had little to say.

Lena glared at me and blew out more smoke. I reached for a cigarette and lit it, but did not inhale.

I touched her hand, but she pulled away and sat with her back to me for several minutes. Then she cut a hole in the paper bag and exhaled into it, the puffs drifting toward the ceiling like smoke signals, as if she thought the smoke would float out into the world, and that our parents would see it, her private signal that she was thinking of them.

I had no such illusions.

It was after we finished the Lorna Doones and I had set the teacups in the top shelf of the dishwasher that I heard Ernie at the door. Lena smiled weakly as I took her hand and led her into the front hall. She had trouble with doorways and often needed to stand behind me to block out the open space hurtling toward her front door.

"Happy birthday," Ernie said, holding his hat over his heart and doing an odd little bow. "Special delivery today for the birthday girl."

I smiled at Ernie as he stepped inside and handed Lena the envelope. I always typed the cards on the computer, using different fonts, careful not to repeat them from year to year. She held the envelope in her fingers and looked up at Ernie and then at me, her eyes shining.

"You think this could be it?" she asked, with a catch in her voice. "You think they really remembered?"

I winked at Ernie and set his mailbag on the floor beside the sofa.

"One never knows," I said, as she rubbed her hands on her lap.

"Go on," Ernie said. "Open it."

She ripped open the envelope with her fingernail and tossed it over her shoulder. Then she lit a cigarette and opened the card:

Dear Lena,
We may have left you, but that does not makes us bad people.
Or does it?
One never knows, does one?
Love,
Ma & Our Father

We said nothing for a long time, and I wondered if I'd taken things too far. But the fact was, with my throbbing head and this newly formed bump, it had taken everything I had to go through with sending the card this year. Ernie understood. When I'd met him on his mail route to hand the card over, he said, "You've gone beyond the call, Cass. No one can say you haven't."

Finally, she put the card down on the coffee table and wrapped her arms around me. I could feel her breath on my neck, shallow and moist, the warmth of the cigarette smoke twirling up through my hair.

"Happy birthday," I said, and she nodded into my neck.

I served the chocolate cake with its gluey white frosting, and we ate it silently, the card hidden under the *TV Guide*.

When we finished, Ernie reached over and kissed Lena's cheek before showing himself to the door. He left the two pieces of cake on the welcome mat with plastic forks on each plate.

"You never know," he said.

Lena smiled and settled on the sofa, clicking on the set with the remote control.

"Right," I added. "One never knows."

I cleared away the plates and remaining cake before settling in next to her to watch the Home Shopping Network and placed the card on the coffee table in front of us. When an Elvis doll appeared on the screen for sale, I looked down at my forged card and felt at the bit of raised flesh beneath my bangs.

Styrofoam, I told myself, as we curled up beside each other on the sofa, our knees touching. How in the hell had styrofoam found a way to climb inside my head?

Later we lay in the twin beds Lena had kept from our childhood and listened to each other breathe. When she married Boyd, I moved to a duplex across town, and Lena and Boyd moved into our parents' old bedroom. They bought out my half of the house, which we'd managed to pay off over the years, and for a while, Lena had even been persuaded to keep most of the family furniture in storage. Once Boyd left her for the dental hygienist, she set up our old bedroom just as it had been when we were kids. Besides the furniture, our parents had left behind almost nothing when they'd disappeared that night, and the few things they did leave had shed little light on where they'd gone. But Lena clung to them—sometimes, I thought, more tightly as the years passed.

As I lay there in the twin bed under flannel sheets, I thought about the bump on my forehead.

"Cass?" Lena whispered in the darkness. "Do you think this means they're never coming back?"

I wanted to give her hope, but really, what was there for them to come back to?

I took a deep breath and rolled onto my side, my sticky bangs pressing into the pillow. It had been a struggle, keeping up with Lena's needs all these years. Her internet shrink sessions were expensive, and once Boyd had left and her agoraphobia had forced her to quit the post office, getting by from month to month had been difficult at times. Ma had left the numbers of bank accounts to draw from, and Our Father had bought us bonds that came due periodically. I'd dole out the money for extra supplies—medications, cigarettes, off-season holiday decorations.

Lena always managed to do enough home telemarketing or data entry to get by, but I'd borne the brunt of their departure—something I'm sure they knew would happen, and if I ever find them, if I have the inclination, I will tell them how terribly unfair they had been, sneaking off in the night.

"One can never tell," I said, and we said good-night, my forehead tingling as I thought of Ma raking her bare scalp with a comb in front of a full-length mirror, Our Father sipping scalding coffee in a brand-new mug. If I'd known where they were and that I'd soon have a six-inch horn on my head, I'd have sent them a poofy black wig on a styrofoam head to remind them of the pain they'd caused poor Lena.

THREE

WHAT THEY LEFT BEHIND

1. a string of Ma's dental floss in the bathroom wastebasket
2. a petrified wand of mascara
3. the pen Ma had used to write her good-bye letter
4. a ticket to an Elvis concert dated one week after his death
5. an old belt buckle worn by Our Father
6. a clump of Ma's dyed black hair
7. a nail clipper with the jagged edges of a toenail still stuck to the tiny blades (we believed the toenail to be Our Father's but were not sure)
8. a yellowed newspaper clipping of Elvis in his coffin from the *National Enquirer* with the word "Bastards" written across his face
9. an unwashed coffee mug of Our Father's
10. a copy of the book, *Elvis, What Happened?,* by Elvis's bodyguards, with clumps of pages torn out
11. broken pieces of an old Mamas and the Papas album
12. the game Twister, still in its original box
13. an empty bottle of black hair dye
14. a sheet of paper with the words "Fuck the Colonel" in Our Father's handwriting
15. our birth certificates
16. a sympathy card addressed to the Presley family postmarked "Return to Sender"

Lena had numbered the items and guarded them, setting them around the house like shrines. On the coffee table, Our Father's mug sat unwashed. Traces of his saliva could still be found in that cup, Lena said, though after so long, all I'd ever seen was a blackish mold that had grown along the bottom where the coffee grains had all but disintegrated.

She'd had me laminate the newspaper clippings and cards, and she kept the toenail clipper, dental floss, and a few of the other items in jars in her bedroom.

We knew right away that the number sixteen was significant. Sixteen items for a man who died alone in the bathroom on the sixteenth day of August.

It's morbid, I know. But then again, so were our parents.

In the morning I got up before the alarm and went directly to the shower. Lena was still asleep. At night, she said, the "dark thoughts" came, and there was little she could do to stop them. Night after night she went through a ritual of what she called her "Funeral Fantasies." First she'd imagine Ma's funeral, which always featured a cherrywood casket and pallbearers from the life we'd drummed up for Ma—faceless women with dental floss tied in little bows around their teeth who knitted afghans and hummed Elvis's version of "How Great Thou Art." They whispered to each other about how well Ma looked in death, how black and full her hair had become after all the years of thinning, all the treatments she'd tried.

Ma had never had many friends. I think she must have had some at one point in her life: fellow fans, women from the bars smelling of beer where Rusty performed and Our Father kept the scarves and water flowing. Or women from the neighborhood, mothers of classmates of Lena's and mine, but since I remember so little of my early childhood except for Elvis, none of them come to mind.

Next Lena would imagine her own funeral, which she said was sketchy, just her body in a plain box lain out by the bay window near her front porch. Ernie would place flowers on the casket, and someone would sing an old Mamas and the Papas song. (She was careful never to mention if this person was in fact me, since she knew how I felt about the Mamas and the Papas.) Then came Our Father's, a memorial service held in a local church. A priest handed out strands of Ma's hair and murmured lines from Elvis's "King Creole" about catfish jumping from a pole and coming from New Orleans. In Lena's fantasies, Our Father had been blown to smithereens—vaporized, she said, nothing left of him but a sooty gold belt buckle with his initials on it.

With all the time she spent on these fantasies, it was no wonder she had such trouble falling asleep at night.

The last funeral was mine. At first she begged off when I asked her what she saw, as if afraid that telling me might bring about my death. Finally, though, she said that all she could see of it were the throngs of people who came, people she'd never seen before in long black coats and gloves to cover their hands, and that my casket was closed because something terrible had happened to my face.

"Like what?" I asked her. "An accident?"

She shook her head and lowered her voice.

"No, nothing like that," she said. "I don't know what it is. It's just that you're not as beautiful as you used to be, and nobody can bear to see you that way."

I thought about waking her and asking if she'd had my funeral fantasy, if she had some insight into what had happened to my head, especially since the bump had kept me awake most of the night. She was keen with her predictions, most of the time, though people rarely listened to her. I decided to let her sleep. She rarely got up before ten since the medication she took left her groggy and unfocused until noon.

I thought of calling Maureen, the owner of the spa, Regal Restoration, to tell her I wouldn't be in that day, but one of our regulars, a woman we called Cousin It, was scheduled for one of her all-day appointments. She came in once a month to have her extensions reworked and lengthened. In the beginning we'd covered up the thinning patches by attaching small hair additions with a series of clips and given her a soft bob, blunt at the edges, no scalp showing through, but she'd gotten so carried away by the idea of having hair again that she'd insisted on extensions that hung below her waist.

Women got that way sometimes, Maureen reminded me when one of the other aestheticians or I referred to her as Cousin It. Maureen called it "The Rapunzel Effect."

I called it neurosis. And I've never heard of any "Rapunzel Effect" before or since.

Cousin It wore the extensions stringy with cheap gels and had a stomach that melded into blobs along her back and hips. Selena, one of the massage therapists, had to soak her hands in hot towels after working on her because kneading that kind of flesh caused her carpal tunnel syndrome to flare up.

"*Oy*, Cass, you don't know the knots in my hands," Selena would say. "That you should never know from such knots!"

Selena coached me on Yiddish words whenever we had spare time. Since she knew I'd always wanted to become a Jew, she'd taught me a variety of phrases: *shmatte, goyim, shmuck, yente.* Many of our clients suffering from hair loss were Jewish, and it was always helpful to throw in a *mazel tov* when a woman achieved a whole new look.

I do take the word "suffering" very seriously when it comes to this subject, in spite of Ma's own history.

I once asked Selena how to say "Rapunzel" in Yiddish, and she said, "Listen to me, *mammele.* That girl is no Rapunzel."

Maureen insisted we give Cousin It the best treatment possible since she was a regular client and good tipper. Selena always said that Maureen had the heart of a *shikse* but the business sense of a good Jewish woman.

She meant this as a high compliment.

Once a month Cousin It had a "Jour de Beauté": facial, massage, pedicure, and makeup application, as if she were continuously off to a prom or practicing to be the bride she one day hoped to become.

Joan, who supervised the computer imaging at Regal's, had the worst job of all. Every month Cousin It arrived with her hair untwined and frizzed from French braiding it, which caused more hair loss at the base of her head and around her forehead. Joan would then do a reconsultation, which Cousin It always insisted upon, and Joan would point out the reasons why it made little sense to continue having me implement such long extensions since they pulled at her scalp and exacerbated her problems.

But Cousin It would shake her head and smile primly at the computer printout of herself in a chestnut shag with full sides and a cropped angle around her face.

"It needs to be long," she always said. "You wouldn't understand."

Of course she was right. There was so little any of us understood about hair loss. We knew the facts, but we hadn't suffered the way our clients had. We didn't have to watch our shiny hair fall away with little we could do to stop it. We could help restore their looks, at least partly, but we could never know how it felt to sit in that chair and see our own hairless and pitiful expressions staring back at us.

I knew what it was like watching Ma grow sadder and sadder as more of her hair fell out, and maybe that was partly why I was secretly relieved when she up and left us.

As usual, Lena had left her arc of negative thoughts pasted to the mirror. Her internet shrink once told her it was important to exorcize her negative thoughts (or was it *exercise?*). At first she'd written them down in notebooks that she kept hidden under her bed, but then he suggested that she use those little sticky notes and paste them around the house.

She used to leave them everywhere—on kitchen cabinets, windows, the refrigerator door—but then she started posting them on lamp shades. After I mentioned that they might pose a fire hazard, she moved them exclusively to the bathroom mirror. And instead of limiting herself to yellow, which she thought too drab, she moved on to rainbow-colored notes— neon greens, aquamarines, lavenders, and indigos.

It was somewhat more cheerful, I'll admit, but not much. Especially since I was trying to examine the growing lump on my head.

When I looked at myself in the mirror that morning, my face was framed in the arc of her notes:

If I had it to do over again, I'd have taken one of her notes and written underneath the last line: *I do, Lena. I do.*

I stepped into the shower and turned the water on, letting the hot needles prick my skin and leave long streaks down my breasts. Normally I shampooed first before attending to the more delicate parts of my body, but that day I soaped up quickly under my arms and between my legs then patted a glob of shampoo—a cheap brand I would never have normally used—on the top of my head. I massaged my scalp and tried to wash away the heaviness of leftover dreams about Our Father and Elvis bent over on the Twister board, Ma reaching frantically over them and shrieking, "Left Hand, Green!" When I was about to rinse off, I lathered my face with soap and let my fingers move slowly from my chin to my nose and finally over my forehead.

It had grown.

I switched off the tap and reached for the towel, my eyes burning from soap and lack of sleep. The mirror was full of steam as I stepped out of the shower and piled a towel on top of my head, the only thing visible were the points of my breasts peeking through the small circles of glass that hadn't been clouded over. I scrubbed a space clean with a tissue then leaned forward against the counter, bits of lint adhering to the mirror in crazy circles.

As my face grew clearer, I saw it there pressing out at my skin from inside, the bump turning a deep pink with the force of its attempt to emerge. Everyone had always complimented me on the quality of my skin. It had the perfect balance of natural oil and elasticity, without even the hint of a fine line under my eyes. I was the prettiest employee Maureen had ever had, she always told me, and natural beauty like mine was the best kind of advertising. It made the clients think that the right combination of extensions and additions could make them look like me—not to mention the use of our other services like seaweed treatments or paraffin wax. She depended on me to look my best. And I wasn't one to let people down.

Having a horn—even the beginnings of a horn—is no excuse to let yourself go.

I swabbed at the raised area with baby powder since that's all Lena had, over and over again until there was a pasty white dot just above my eyebrow line that made me look like a Hindu ghost. If we finished with Cousin It early, I thought, slapping at the bump with a powder puff, I could have Stella give me a seaweed mask and a mud bath to get the swelling down.

As if that would have helped.

FOUR

My mother named Lena and me after the singers she'd heard
playing on the car radio on the way to the hospital each time
she was in labor. The agreement was that if we were boys, Our
Father would have chosen the names, but since we were, of
course, girls, Ma tried to compromise as best she could. On
the day Lena was born, Ma happened to catch Lena Horne
singing "Stormy Weather" on an oldies station, and I was
named "Cass" for Mama Cass of the Mamas and the Papas,
who happened to be on the car radio as soon as they flipped
on the switch. Ma left it to chance, though I always felt she
could have given the choice some more thought. For much of
my childhood I fought to be Cassandra instead of Cass,
though my atrocious grammar-school spelling and the name
on all my school records squashed that rather quickly. I've
always thought that Ma's radio dialings should have been
reversed—for many reasons, my horn being the most recent.
After all, Lena's been prone to weight problems all her life,
and I was the pretty one with my straight teeth, a tannish
glow to my skin.

We've spent much of our lives cursing Ma's leaving the
decision to chance, though I've often told Lena it could have
been much worse if we'd been boys. If Our Father had done
the naming, one of us could have been Elvis. Not that I resent
the King, despite our parents' obsession, but Elvis is not the
kind of name to be easily carried by a middle-class white boy
from suburbia.

Lena could have been named "Gladys" for Elvis's mother because Ma felt bad about Our Father's losing his first time out, but Our Father didn't accept her concession. We didn't know which one of them had collected the Elvis clippings and snatches of memorabilia or if it was something they'd come upon together. Lena has always thought Our Father truly worshipped him and that Ma just went along with it. After all, he'd been the roadie, and Ma had been just another woman in the audience at Rusty's shows. I tend to believe the obsession was Ma's since she seemed to make most of the decisions in the house and gave Our Father high marks for his efforts with Rusty. In all likelihood, though, it was something they shared—one of the many things they kept between them.

Theirs was a symbiotic relationship if ever there was one. "Symbiotic" was a favorite word of Vance's—one I've come to love, despite all that has since happened with him.

I spent my childhood terrified of eating ham sandwiches. Luckily Ma seemed to sense this and never offered them as school lunches, though at play dates with other kids, I was forced to confront them. The first time this happened, I was in second grade, and my friend Yvonne invited me to her house for lunch one day. There on my plate sat a ham on rye, dry, no condiments, which made the anxiety all the more intense. Easily chokeable. I picked at the crust until finally Yvonne's mother asked me what was wrong with the sandwich. At seven, I couldn't explain my fear of death to a mother I hardly knew, let alone admit I'd been named for a singer who had choked on a sandwich just like the one in front of me.

"I can't eat ham," I blurted, refusing to look at either the sandwich or at Yvonne's mother. "I'm not allowed."

Yvonne's mother laughed nervously and yanked the plate away.

"Oh, you're Jewish," she said, blushing slightly as she hurried to fix me some peanut butter and jelly. "How silly of me not to realize."

I nodded furiously and ate the peanut butter without ever looking up. Yvonne, who had no idea what it meant to be Jewish, was horrified to learn I wasn't going to be in the Christmas pageant at school.

"You mean you can't have Santa Claus?" she asked.

I shrugged and smacked the peanut butter with my tongue. She'd seen my Christmas tree the year before, I was sure of it, so I swallowed hard and said, "Yeah, but only half."

"She must be Sephardic with that coloring," I heard her mother whisper. After that day I begged Ma for menorahs and cut Jewish stars out of construction paper to hang on my bedroom walls. Better to fake being Jewish than to admit I'd been terrorized by my namesake's untimely death, that I forever feared a glob of ham being caught in my throat while I turned purple and fought for breath. Even now, all these years later, I've adopted something of a kosher diet, declaring pork and Spam against my religion even though I don't have much use for God.

Our Father was the only person besides Lena that I ever confided these fears in, and when I did, he laughed and laughed.

"So does that mean if we'd named you Elvis you would've refused to take prescription medication?" he asked.

We were sitting in the living room when I made my confession. He was smoking a cigarette, a yellowed toenail poking through a hole in his white sock. I remember looking over at Lena, who was poring over the inscriptions in her yearbook and copying them into a notebook. She needed to be reminded constantly of what people had thought of her.

"I guess that's what it means, yes," I said, as he stubbed out his cigarette and turned on the television.

Three days later, they were gone.

Our parents left on the tenth anniversary of Elvis's death—August 16th, 1987. You may find this coincidental—and I'm not altogether sure it's not—though Lena and I have our own theories. Some of them I'll share. Some are between my sister and me.

Sometimes we think they were convinced Elvis was alive, and at other times we're sure they accepted his death. When the stories first started circulating about Elvis being spotted at fast food joints in Kalamazoo, Our Father bought a book that insisted Elvis had faked his death. I found the book one night after he'd come home with his trunk filled with Rusty's scarves and I read it under the covers with a flashlight. The writer insisted that the thousands of fans at Graceland had filed past a wax figure cooled by a giant air conditioning unit. The book came with a bonus tape recording of Elvis telling some unnamed but trusted confidante that he'd wanted to escape his life.

I never got to ask Our Father whether he believed this theory, but whether he did or not, it would certainly seem that Our Father wanted to escape his life, too.

I've never believed that Elvis is alive. I was sure, even then, that Elvis would never have left his daughter no matter how much fame had imprisoned him.

We've often wondered why they chose the tenth anniversary and didn't wait around until the fifteenth or even the twentieth, when we were out of the house and settled. It does no good to torment ourselves on this issue, though, as I've told Lena many times, even if she refuses to listen.

Lena was nineteen then and I'd just started hairdressing school—they've since changed the name to "School of Aesthetics and Hair Care," which pleases me. We were two young women ready to make our way in the world, as it were, when our parents one-upped us and moved out before we had the chance.

Family life had never been particularly troublesome, though Ma did have problems with her hair beginning to fall out and then dyeing it black, which only accentuated the rapid appearance of her scalp. I'd bought her wigs from time to time—always blond, as it was a color much better suited to her creamy skin—but she refused to wear them.

"They itch," she said, "and going bald is bad enough."

Our Father, of course, never did make it to Vegas, as he and Rusty had dreamed, and he'd been born tone deaf, leaving hopes of his own career as an impersonator long dashed. He did make a good living as a machinist at a belt buckle manufacturer, and Ma sold cosmetics on the side. Looking back, I realize they had always lived in a state of low-grade miserableness, a kind of quiet malaise, but nothing that could have foretold their disappearance that night, or the note that followed:

Dear Cass & Lena,

You'll notice in the morning that we're gone. Don't expect us to return. You might be tempted to try and find us, but it would be better for all of us if you didn't.

Life seems to be getting away from us, and it's time we found it. You girls are old enough to understand and get by on your own. You'll find money in a bank account in both of your names, which we hope will allow you to remember us with some fondness. If you'd rather forget us, that's fine, too.

You girls never really understood us, and I doubt we ever understood you, either. We hoped you'd love the things that we loved. But you didn't. What have we ever really done for you but give you names you don't seem to understand or appreciate and maybe a few good memories? You've never given us any heartache. Maybe it would have been better if you had. Still, it's too late for any of that.

Your father is loading the car as I write this. We thought it best not to wake you to say good-bye. Lena is too fragile for that kind of emotion, anyway.

And don't beat yourselves up. There would have been no talking us out of this.

Cass and Lena, you have each other now. At least we gave you that much. We have hopes for both of you, though they may not have been high enough.

We may be in touch, and then again, we may not.

With all the love we have,
Ma & Dad

The next day, when we found the note, Lena opened her mouth and screamed for a full fifteen minutes. But I said nothing, just crumpled the note into a ball and held my hands over my ears until she stopped.

FIVE

On my way to Regal Restoration, which we had all shortened to "Regal's" over time, I stopped at my house for a pretty lace cap I had bought when I let one of the other specialists cut my bangs in spikes for a show a few years earlier. The model we hired called last-minute with the stomach flu, and I had to be the stand-in. No one else would do it—not even Rose, Lena's pedicurist who gelled her hair so thick you could balance a book on it and was the one person on our staff who could have used a change. The spikes complemented the eighties line of makeup that was in that year, lots of black eyeliner and thick lines of peach blush called Coral Fun, but at home I wore baseball hats and this particular lacy cap for six months while it grew out to a chin-length bob.

Little did I know then how often I'd eventually be wearing hats. For a while I let people think I was having chemo, tucking my hair inside the cap so you could see only a tuft in the back. I hid it for as long as I could.

But you can only hide a horn for so long.

As I did on most mornings, I went to Bagel King for a cinnamon bagel with cream cheese and lox. The guys behind the counter would stop what they were doing when I came in, nudging each other and making faces at me. I found the whole display rather repulsive, actually, and the only reason I kept coming in was that the bagels were the best within a twenty-five-mile radius.

A rabbi had told me about Bagel King in line at another bagel store, and I had never forgotten it.

"Bagel King," he'd said. "Harry Stein's place. Best bagels and bialys you'll ever have."

I peered in at the flat, misshapen bagels I'd just bought lying against each other in the paper bag.

"And the lox?" I whispered.

He raised his eyebrows at me, obviously impressed that a *shikse* like myself should speak of lox. I had a sudden urge to ask him to quote something from the Torah and to confess my terrifying fear of ham to him, but his voice in my ear calmed me.

"The lox," he said, "oh, not the lox. They wouldn't know good lox at this place if it hit them in the head like a stone."

He leaned in so closely that I felt his breath in my ear.

"I'm only here because I'm doing a Bar Mitzvah for the owner, and we have an obligation to patronize."

I threw out my bagels in the parking lot and drove straight to Bagel King that day, even though it took me fifteen more minutes to get to Regal's from there.

They were waiting for me when I arrived, hands on their apron strings, eyes darting. A crowd of heavily perfumed women pressed in front of me, grabbing their numbers and calling out orders. I reached forward for my number and held it in the palm of my hand.

Sixteen—the date of Elvis's death.

There was no getting away from it.

When my turn finally came, a balding man in his late thirties stood at the counter with his pencil in hand. I handed him my number and looked up at the ceiling.

"Ah, Sixteen," he said. "Sweet Sixteen. You should be Number One, but Sixteen, well, that number is sweet. How are you, Sixteen? Where were you yesterday, Sixteen?" He eyed my breasts through my dress and didn't even seem to notice the cap.

What a nudnik, I thought. *A real* putz.

I would never tell them my name, and they'd learned to stop asking, calling me by number only.

"Birthday party," I said, not looking at him. It was so tiring, all those eyes on me all the time, at the post office, the deli counter, the husbands picking up their full-haired wives after treatments at Regal's. Even when I'd drag myself out of bed at night to go to the convenience store for Lena, some pimply-faced teenager would ogle me in my T-shirt and sweats when all I wanted was a carton of cigarettes and some diet soda and to be left alone. And that was *before* the horn.

"Your birthday, Sixteen?" he asked. "Don't tell me you turned sixteen."

He laughed so hard that spittle flew from his mouth and landed on the countertop. He was so busy staring at me that he didn't even wipe it away.

"No, my sister's," I said. "Can I have a sesame seed with light cream cheese and lox? I'm running late."

He looked down at my number and then at his hands.

"Certainly, Sixteen. To make a bagel for a beauty like you is an honor for a man like me."

I mumbled a thanks and felt my throat burn, the bump pulsing beneath the cap.

When I finished paying and took the bagel in the paper bag from him, he reached over and ran a finger over the slope of my knuckles.

"Pleasure to serve you, Sixteen," he said. "I'll serve you any way I can, Sixteen."

I waved a hand behind me and hurried out to the car, where I ate the bagel as quickly as I could. At the last bite, I thought of his saliva splattered on the counter, and the lox came back up. I spat it out the window, leaving a blob of pinkness on the yellow line of my parking space. Lox had never sickened me before, but now it felt lodged in my throat. I imagined tiny scales clinging to my esophagus.

Although I didn't know it then, I would never return to Bagel King after that day. I would never eat lox again. And the looking—the constant eyes on me—would only get worse.

When I got to Regal's, Cousin It was sitting in her white robe and slippers sipping mineral water. I smelled the peppermint lotion and polish fresh from her pedicure. She liked to come in early and enjoy the services we provided, taking her time downstairs at the manicure/pedicure stations, thrilling in a massage in the quiet area of the spa until finally arriving upstairs at the private stations where the actual additions took place. Aside from the freakishly long outdated hair, I had to give her credit for stringent maintenance. Her polish never chipped, and her toenails were always filed and neatly trimmed. Joan saw me come in as I passed Cousin It and made my way up the stairs, waved me into the back office and closed the door behind us.

"Did you get a look at her?" she asked, lighting aromatherapy candles to mask the smell of the neutralizers we used for power perms. "That's enough hair for forty people. This is not the kind of client who's good for business."

She looked at herself in the mirror and fluffed the layers in her hair with her fingertips.

"Some people would kill for that hair," I said, pulling the brim lower on my forehead.

"I don't know who," she said.

I had a brief vision of my mother, balding, standing outside the dumpster of a hair salon and fishing in the garbage for shorn locks.

"Every time it's the same thing with her," she said. "I print out a picture of her in a bob, a shag, a normal style. Normal," she repeated. She blew out the aromatherapy candle then straightened her skin-tight minidress. We all wore heels and short dresses, even in winter. "Listen, when you're working on her today, try to talk her into letting go of those extensions. It's unseemly in a place like this."

Maureen knocked on the door and leaned her head in. She was always solicitous of me, never chastising me for running late or for talking about my mother's hair loss to the clients. Usually this was forbidden. Every woman's hair loss was hers and hers alone, she always said, but with me, she made an exception.

"Cass, your client is waiting for you," she said. She looked at the cap and smiled. "Oh, did you cut your hair?"

I shook my head and mouthed to Joan, *I've got something to show you,* before she stepped out, but she didn't catch it since her back was turned as she closed the door behind her.

"Good Luck!" Joan called, and I slipped into my white jacket. I could feel Maureen looking at me, but I didn't turn around.

While my next client was having her computer consult with Joan, I got ready to start on Cousin It. Her real name was Crystal, after Crystal Gale, sister of Loretta Lynn—and unlike me, she did everything in her power to live up to her name. It would make anyone's brown eyes blue to think about it.

She always asked for the same regimen, no matter what suggestions I offered. I'd tried time and again to get her to allow me to experiment with other hair addition techniques—a mix of weaves and falls to draw the eye away from her fatty chin and accent the sharp angle of her cheekbones—but all she ever wanted was to keep the extensions and to add more length to the bottom.

"You think you're up to this?" Maureen finally asked. "You look tired, Cass."

I'd managed to keep from facing her while she was talking, but had to turn toward her to get to my station.

"Sure," I said. "I could do Cousin It in my sleep."

She winced at my use of the nickname but said nothing.

Maureen, I suspected, had always been a bit afraid of me, but I didn't yet know why.

Most people wish to inspire love, devotion, even worship in people. I guess Elvis felt that way.

But there's one thing most people never think about—to know how it feels to have that kind of beauty stare you in the face. Not just to appreciate beauty, the way most people do, but to have it as your own.

To own it.

I wonder if Elvis felt the pressure of his own beauty weighing down on him, if in those last years when he seemed not to care anymore, or was at least resigned to having lost his looks, if he felt somehow unburdened. He did seem to love the glitz and glamour of being Elvis with his rhinestone jumpsuits and gold belts.

Even when his face had grown distorted, he still tried to look as beautiful as he could for the people who loved him.

But what, I wonder, did he want? Did he hope his fans saw more than that face? Or did he wish it had never changed?

Or did he do it all to himself because he didn't want to be beautiful anymore?

When Maureen was gone I collapsed in a chair and took several deep breaths before finding the courage to look in the mirror again. My skin was pale with bluish circles under my eyes. Beads of sweat formed under the rim of the cap and ran down my nose. I powdered my entire face and swabbed more concealer under my eyes with a wedge. The cap itched, and I felt at the bump underneath, a hard raised ball now, like an egg. I was tempted, but I didn't look.

Instead I hurried out to greet Cousin It and asked her how she'd been since I'd last seen her.

"The thing is, with my kind of job," she said, "I have to look good, and that's not always so easy."

I fingered my Filofax as I opened the tray of extensions, searching her card for what it was she did for a living. But all it said was "hospital attendant."

I laid out the array of clips and woven strands of hair and forced a smile.

"It must take a lot of energy," I said, setting out my pins and hanging the extensions on tiny hooks, "trying to look healthy for all those sick people."

As she smiled, I saw the face of Mama Cass staring out at me as if from the cover of her album. I half-expected her to launch into "Monday, Monday" and start swaying dreamily at my station.

"It's not looking healthy that's important where I work," she whispered. "It's looking normal that counts."

That was the goal of Regal's, the one quality that baldness stripped women of, Maureen always said. Normalcy. I was beginning to know what that meant.

Visions of mental patients strapped in straitjackets flashed through my head, Lena in a recreation room writing out her negative thoughts in large black letters on construction paper and holding them up for Cousin It to see. Several of the combs on my station tumbled to the floor.

"But who knows what normal is, anymore, right?" she laughed. "I mean, you can never really tell who's normal these days."

I smiled then and adjusted one of the extensions wrapped around the tufts of natural hair at her scalp, subtly, with just a slight twist of my comb, while she wasn't looking.

"Yes, exactly," I said. "One never knows."

In any other case I would have tried to explain that someone with her sallow skin and thick eyebrows should have had all the extensions removed and focus on the thinning areas, but instead I tightened the weaves and lengthened the ends with extensions twisted throughout the length of her hair. By the time I was finished, the hair came down below her buttocks.

If I hadn't done the work myself, I wouldn't have believed it.

When I was finished, she smiled in the mirror, and blotted her lipstick with a tissue. I bent down to put the extra strands of hair back inside the cases when I felt her looking at me.

For a minute she sat there looking at me and then gripped my elbow.

"What's that on your head?" she whispered.

I straightened up to look in the mirror and saw that the cap had ridden up, revealing the bump, now the size of a half-dollar. Pale face powder was caked over it, creating a large beige bull's-eye in the middle of my forehead. I pulled the cap down as fast as I could and looked away.

When Cousin It/Crystal was finished, she stopped at my station to hand me the envelope with my tip inside and beamed. As if on cue, Joan, the other replacement specialists, and I broke into a collective smile. The cap squeezed my head so tightly I thought my brain would burst, but I waved as she sashayed out the front door, the hair swaying back and forth against the middle of her thighs.

"She looks like a freak," someone said. "Why doesn't somebody tell her?"

I moisturized my hands and thought of the searing way she'd stared at the lump on my head.

"She doesn't have it easy," I said, "working with *meshuggers* all day."

"Really?" one of the manicurists asked, leaning in toward me. "She works with the nuts?"

I nodded.

"Ah, the poor girl," Selena said. "Not only to deal with people who are *meshuge,* Selena said, giving me the eye as she corrected me, "but not to let it get to her. That takes *moxie.*"

She nodded toward the pen on the countertop.

"That girl," she said, "is a *gutte neshuma* under all those extensions. Wouldn't hurt a fly."

I wrote it down, sounding it out.

Gu-teh-ne-shu-ma.

"Get it?" she asked.

I scratched at the bump beneath my cap with the pen's dull end.

"I think so," I said, smiling at Selena. "She's a good person, even though she may not look so hot."

Selena laughed and pinched my cheek.

"I'm still such a *goy*, as hard as I try, right?" I asked.

She smiled and headed back to her station.

"Don't you worry, *mammele*," she called to me. "Your time will come."

Maureen closed the door behind Crystal—Cousin It *gutte neshuma* who worked with *meshuge* people—and wiped at her eyes, smearing eyeliner down the side of her face. I touched my cap and tried to see past her into the mirror on the far wall, but one of the other replacement specialists was in the way, blow-drying a wig that had just been highlighted.

"There's something about that woman that just hits me right here." Maureen clenched a fist over her chest, eyes tearing. "Even the women who suffer through chemo or radiation," she said, "they don't get to me like she does. And I don't know why."

We all laughed for a minute—poor Maureen, she was such a pushover for homely women—and then Joan tugged at my sleeve and pulled me to the back room. She closed the door behind us and stuck a swivel chair in front of it, reaching into the pocket of her smock. I breathed a sigh of relief as she pulled out the joint I knew was waiting there—we often got high after Cousin It sessions—but instead she pointed the joint toward me like an accusation.

"Come on," she said. "Let's see it."

If you only knew how many times I've since heard that line. Some people even think it's original.

When I didn't say anything at first, she handed me the joint. Joan's supplier was a long-time client who'd undergone multiple cycles of chemotherapy and used it for nausea. She gave Joan joints as tips and told Maureen that looking well and feeling well were relative terms. When Maureen suggested that pot smoking went against the ideas of wellness that the spa embraced, the woman said, "I'll give you wellness. Try looking at yourself bald in the mirror and see if it doesn't make you want to get high."

After that, Maureen gave us permission to smoke, but only if we promised to be discreet and only when we were finished for the day.

"How did you know?" I asked, pulling the smoke into my lungs and checking in the mirror to see if the bump was protruding through the cap.

She took the joint back and let the smoke drift up by her face.

"I saw you with Cousin It," she said. "I knew you had to be hiding something under there."

She motioned to the cap and placed one hand on her hip, her red manicured nails stark against the tight-fitting floral dress she was wearing. The rest of us kept our nails short and coated in clear polish, but Joan had been there the longest and demanded to be different.

I peeled the rim of the cap upward, sliding it toward the back of my head and letting it fall to the floor. She set the joint in the ashtray and stood behind me while we both looked.

My lacquered bangs stood straight in the air, the rest of my hair damp and mussed. White clumps of powder clung to the center of what now appeared to be a red rim with scaly bits of skin circling the edges.

"What the hell did you *do?*" she said, turning me around by the shoulders to face her. "Did that goddamned toe-hacker touch you?"

It did look as if someone had hit me, but worse.

I shook my head and laughed a little. Joan had never liked Vance ever since he'd removed Lena's fourth toenail—her "ring" toe, as Joan put it—at her bedside after a bout with fungus. Of course Vance assumed that the nail would grow back, but with the difficulty of follow-up treatment at home and her resistance to vitamin supplements that made her feel like she was being choked from inside, the nail never did return. Lena didn't care, but Joan had taken the toe incident personally.

"Just because Lena stays in the house and not many people see her toes," Joan insisted, "does not make him less responsible."

Lena had the most beautiful feet, Joan had always said, and she could have had a prosperous career as a foot model if only she'd been able to leave the house. Once she'd tried to hire a photographer to take shots of Lena's feet, but Lena didn't like strangers in the house either, since the house was the one place she felt safe. Women's feet were rarely that lovely, and the toe-hacker clearly had no respect for beauty, Joan said, despite the fact that he was dating me. I didn't tell her that his lack of attention to my looks was what first attracted me to him because I knew she wouldn't understand.

"Of course I didn't show Vance," I said. I reached over and sucked at the joint, then lowered my voice to a whisper. "I don't even know what this is."

She reached up to touch it and then pulled her hand away.

"Go ahead," I said. "It doesn't hurt."

She closed her eyes for a minute then reached up with both hands. She pressed it with her fingertips then squeezed it, looking puzzled, before rubbing the caked powder with her thumb.

"Jesus Christ," she said. "It feels like styrofoam, like one of those styrofoam heads. You know, from school."

"I know," I said, and I felt my throat constrict at the mention of the word. If anyone else knew both me and styrofroam equally well, it was Joan. I reached for the cap and pulled it back on.

"Did you fall?"

I shook my head.

"Eat something different? Use a new foundation?"

No, I said, and no again.

She stared at the space in my cap where she now knew it lurked and tapped her fingernails against her chin.

"Nothing you can think of at all?"

I tucked the back of my hair into the cap.

"Yesterday was Lena's birthday, and we did the whole 'Where Are They Now' thing, but besides that, I've done nothing but stay at Lena's and eat Lorna Doones," I said.

I paused and lowered my head.

"Oh, yeah," I murmured, "there is one thing. I puked up some lox in the parking lot."

Joan shook her head and took one more hit from the joint.

"What is it with you?" she asked. "Someone as beautiful as you are, and you want to be someone else. I just don't get it."

I shrugged and sipped at a bottle of mineral water, trying to drown the fishy taste still lingering at the back of my throat.

Maureen knocked at the door then and said that it was time to close up, that she had a speech to give on the importance of nutritional supplements for women with F.P.B.—Female Pattern Balding.

"You'd better get that looked at," Joan said, pulling off her smock and dusting herself off. She pointed a knowing finger at me. "And not by that toe-hacker, either."

I promised I'd see a dermatologist as soon as possible, but that I had to get home to feed the cat and check in on Lena. Joan agreed not to say anything about it until I gave her the go-ahead, and we gave each other an air-kiss and said good-bye.

When I was sure everyone had gone, I hurried back across the parking lot and opened the back door with my key. Maureen had given the key and the alarm code only to me, and even let me choose the numbers and the code word in case the alarm ever tripped. She said the other girls would choose something silly like a kid's birthday or an anniversary date, but knew that I'd come up with something memorable. I picked the first thing that came to mind—8-16-77, the day of Elvis's death—code word: "King."

"That's certainly in keeping with our name," Maureen said when I told her, though I felt shame rush through my chest. "Did I ever tell you that I met Elvis's hairdresser, Larry Geller, at a party once?"

I nodded; she'd told me many times.

"I went right up to him and complimented the way he kept Elvis's hair and asked him what kinds of products he used, but he just pressed a finger to his lips and smiled at me, 'Trade secrets.'" She'd sighed and said with longing, "Elvis. Now there was a beautiful man. A beautiful but troubled king."

Long live the King, I thought with a sneer, and ran into the spa to punch the numbers, the beeps echoing in the dark room.

I turned on as few of the overhead lights as possible and made my way to the facial room. It was still warm from the heat lamps. I stripped off the cap and my blouse and slid into one of the robes reserved for clients. I grabbed the largest hand mirror I could find, climbed up on the table, and switched on the magnifier. Then, raising the mirror ever-so-slowly, I adjusted it until I found the reflection of the bump dead center, then blinked my eyes.

With one of the warm hand towels, I wiped off the powder and foundation and started to work. Bracing myself, I set the hand mirror on the table beside me and squeezed, digging my fingernails in the way you're never supposed to do, not caring if I gave myself an infection.

Extract, extract, I breathed over and over to myself, but the bump merely squished from side to side, no fluid leaking, not a hint of bacteria trapped under the skin.

"What the hell *are* you?" I whispered, holding the mirror and staring at it for minutes on end. The ridges of my fingernails left deep red slashes on my forehead, dots of capillaries bursting around the bump, which twitched a bit when I touched it, but refused to be removed, no matter how hard I pressed.

Feet had nothing to do with the horn's appearance. People later tried to persuade me to let them rub their feet against the horn, as if it could make bone spurs disappear or lance off corns without the slightest bit of pain. But there was no connection then, and there's no connection now.

If you've got foot problems, I tell people, go see a podiatrist.

Don't expect to stick your feet in my face.

I stopped at Vance's office before going home to feed the cat and check on Lena. The receptionist, Sylvia, told me he was lancing some bunions and that he'd be a while, but after a day with Cousin It and getting high with Joan, I just couldn't go home. Vance loved bunions, I knew, and a good one would sometimes keep him busy for an hour or more, then send him off into rhapsodies about the miracle of healthy feet. The cap felt secure on my head, so I used the office's other line to call home for my messages.

There were four messages from Lena—she averaged as many as five a day. Usually she called once every hour or so, updating me on her internet shrink and how many extra Xanax she'd taken trying to work her way out the front door to water the geraniums on the porch, which I usually did for her. It wasn't that she didn't try. The last one was from Ernie, who said he was concerned that Lena was not having a productive day. She hadn't answered when he called her name through the mail slot and hadn't even thanked him for the *Aloha from Hawaii* DVD he'd given her for her birthday.

"I thought she loved Elvis, Cass," he said. "I was only trying to help."

He wanted to have dinner at Lena's that night and said he'd be stopping by on his route later that day to confirm. We had dinner there every Wednesday night without fail, to give Lena something to look forward to. Lena's fixation on our parents' whereabouts coupled with the latest drama of her missing toenail had done none of us any good, but neither

Ernie nor I knew what else to do for her. We either brought take-out or Ernie would make a casserole, since we didn't want to tax Lena any more than necessary. At the end of the evening, she'd invariably ask me to tell her another story about our parents that she hadn't heard before, and I would spend all day trying to come up with one that would live up to her expectations. Of course none of them did.

I called Lena then to check in on her, in case she hadn't heard from her internet shrink yet or Ernie had been bogged down by the day's mail.

"Hi," I said, when she answered on the first ring, as always. "Did you hear from Ernie? He said you didn't speak to him today. It's Wednesday night."

I could hear Lena sucking in smoke on the other end. She often lost track of days being in the house all the time, and there were a few times when Wednesday suddenly caught her unawares.

"Yeah, he came by again after he dropped off the mail," Lena said. "He's bringing Chinese at seven. I've been anxious all day. More so than usual, I mean."

I could hear the patient's muffled groans coming from Vance's office, the sounds of whistling. Vance always whistled when working on bunions.

"Can you tell me a story about them?" Lena asked. "I need to hear something about them right now. Not even about where they are, but, you know, something I wouldn't remember."

An elderly woman in the corner with open-toed sandals looked at me, her toes wrapped in white tubes for pressing corns. She was staring at my cap, and I pulled it down lower and felt my face flush.

"I'll think of something special," I promised, turning away from the woman and feeling at the raised egg beneath my cap. "But let's save it for tonight."

Vance came out of the office then. The patient hobbled to the receptionist to settle his bill. Vance grinned and motioned for me to come inside, and I held my finger up in the air to signal that I needed a minute. I heard Lena saying my name several times while Vance told the patient to ice his foot for twenty minutes every hour to keep the swelling down.

"Cass?" she asked again. "Cass, will you tell me something important? Something that will help me understand?"

I smiled at the patient, a man in his late forties with a receding hairline, and coughed into the receiver. The man grimaced and dragged his foot on the carpet on his way out the door.

"I'll try," I said weakly, since I didn't see how I could ever help her understand when I had no more insights than she had. "See you later," I said, and hung up before she could say anything else. For a minute I thought about calling back, to talk to her about the bump, as that was something she hadn't heard before, but that might have added to her anxiety, so I thought better of it.

Vance locked me in an embrace in the office and kissed me, his tongue poking around the back of my teeth as if fishing for food I'd forgotten to scrape away. His hardness pressed against the zipper of my jeans as he pushed me up against the wall. My head throbbed.

I managed to free myself and straightened my cap. One look at the egg on my head would calm his erection, I thought, but I'd promised Joan I wouldn't show it to him—at least not yet.

"Oh, Cass," he whispered, nicking my earlobe with his tongue, "one rarely sees bunions like those. I saved that man's feet for sure."

If he could cure feet every day of his life—not counting the removal of Lena's fungal toenail—then maybe, I thought, I should just tear off the cap right there and ask him to get out his lance.

Can you save me? I thought of saying, but didn't.

PART II

[Elvis] is deplorable,
a rancid-smelling aphrodisiac.

—FRANK SINATRA

SIX

Recently I've been thinking of Lena's motto and how it would have applied in my case: W.W.E.D., or What Would Elvis Do? It got her through the worst times in her life, she said, and had never failed her.

(A) He'd have called the Colonel, who would have suggested he go on the road: "Elvis—The Man, the Myth, the Horn."

(B) He'd have learned how to wield it as a karate weapon while practicing moves with the Memphis Mafia.

(C) He'd have made another of his bad movies with rhyming names, like *Harum Scarum* or *Double Trouble*, letting the studios call this one, *Horned and Scorned*.

(D) He'd have concentrated until the horn shot out like a bullet, right through the television sets he was so fond of blasting up.

None of these ideas have helped.

When I got home, the cat, Grizabella, had scratched the back of my futon, the threads hanging in long clumps. She was still a kitten, really, six months old and already in heat. The vet had told me I'd have to keep her inside and wait until it was over before I could have her fixed. She'd taken to rubbing up against my arms at night and growling low in her throat. Once while Vance and I were making love, she jumped on his back and worked herself into a meowing frenzy, raking him with her claws.

"I don't know who was more excited, you or that cat," he said as he rolled off me and stood up to look at the scratches on his back in the mirror.

As I swabbed them with Betadine, I looked over at the sleeping cat and said, "One can never tell."

The sex with Vance was never particularly good, and in fact I was grateful to Griz for helping to add some excitement. Normally Vance would go immediately to the bathroom to wipe himself clean and would then stand in the mirror with his foot on the countertop checking for ingrown toenails. He was prone to them and swore that too much sex brought them out.

Vance had taken to spending more and more time in his makeshift lab, struggling to come up with a formula for replacing toenails that refused to grow back. Lena's was a peculiar case, he always said. Other patients' toenails had enjoyed healthy regrowth after being removed, and the fact that hers did not grow back had confounded him. He rented a small warehouse not far from his office, and though I'd tried to sneak inside several times, the door had always been dead-bolted. It was a labor of love, that lab of his, especially after the travesty of what had happened with Lena's toenail.

"Travesty" was another of Vance's favorite words. Her refusal to wear a plastic prosthetic toenail was an added travesty, he often said.

It's not a word I'd have applied in Lena's case.

At least not where her feet were concerned.

Her toenail was the least of her problems.

Griz followed me into the bedroom and jumped on the bed while I took off my cap and blouse. I needed to lie down, especially before having to tell stories later at Lena's house. My head throbbed, a thick pulse beating in the egg. The smell of Vance's foot chemicals had left a film on me, even coating my hair. Since leaving his office, everything seemed unbearably loud, even the cat's purring.

I sat on the edge of the bed and looked at myself in the mirror on my bureau. Violet circles ringed my eyes. I smoothed a repairing gel under them, trying to make the circles disappear. Vance hadn't said anything about the cap or the circles, and he seemed especially charged up, pinning me against the wall and grinding his hips against me. When I broke away and told him I couldn't see him that night, he looked down at his shoes and said, "Forgive me. I've got to see to some corns."

I didn't know if he was disappointed by my lack of interest or if the image of the old woman's gnarled feet had somehow gotten in the way of his desire, but neither had deterred him before.

Maybe he sensed then that I was changing. But how could he have known?

The bump looked the same as it had earlier that day, except it seemed pinker now that the powder had worn away. I rubbed moisturizer on the scaly rim and dialed the dermatologist's number.

"I have this egg on my head," I told the receptionist, "and I don't know how it got there."

She asked for my name and telephone number and whether I'd been to their office before.

"Once," I said, watching myself in the mirror as I spoke, using one hand to poke at the sides of the bump, "when I had a rash on my behind from sitting on a public toilet."

The receptionist paused as she took down the information. Griz rubbed her bottom against the phone cord and yawned.

"What exactly does this egg look like?" she asked, and then went through the same questions Joan had asked me earlier that day. Already I grew tired of them.

"It looks like an egg, is all I can tell you," I said. "I did throw up some lox today in the parking lot of Bagel King."

I felt at the bump with my fingertip and waited for her response.

"Really?" she asked. "And I've heard such raves about their bagels."

"It does give one pause," I said, "doesn't it?"

She told me to come in the next morning and the doctor would examine it and possibly take a scraping.

"It may be an allergic reaction," she said. "He'll probably do some tests."

I thanked her and hung up the phone. As I lay back against the pillows and closed my eyes to stop the throbbing, Griz came over and sniffed at the bump.

"What is it, Griz?" I asked the cat, stroking her back as she raised her tail in the air. "What do you think happened to my head?"

The cat backed away to the edge of the bed and hissed. Then before I could stop her, she jumped on my face and rubbed herself against it, pushing her behind into the bump and letting out a rumbling growl. I tried to throw her off, but she dug her bottom into my face and held onto either side of my head with both claws. When I finally managed to peel her paws from my head, she sat at the edge of the bed and glared at me, her mouth open slightly, as if she were laughing.

When your own cat turns against you, it's a warning that's hard to ignore.

I stopped at the store to buy Lena toilet paper and a carton of cigarettes. The supermarket delivered most of her essentials, but one could never have too much toilet paper or cigarettes, I thought. At the checkout counter, a kid with whiteheads and pockmarks made loud sniffing noises.

"You sure smell good," he said, rattling the plastic bag as he shoved the cigarettes and toilet paper inside. "What's that you're wearing?"

I lifted my wrist to my nose and sniffed. I'd forgotten to wear perfume that day, something I'd never done, not as long as I could remember. It had to be the remnants of Vance's chemicals.

"I'll bet it's just you," he said, and smiled, flashing a row of silver braces.

Without answering, I grabbed the bag and stormed out the door, bells jangling above my head as it closed behind me. In the car I set the bag on the passenger seat and sniffed at my wrist again, even lifted my arm to check for underarm odor.

He was right. Whatever it was, it was just me.

When I got to the house, Ernie's mail truck was in the driveway. I stopped to hook up the hose to water the begonias and geraniums, which were wilted and browning fast from too much sun.

Inside I laid the plastic bag down on the kitchen table and straightened my baseball cap with the Elvis logo on it: T.C.B.

with a lightning bolt, a gift from Lena. *Taking Care of Business in a Flash*. She'd ordered it from the Graceland catalog she received each month in the mail. It was one of the few Elvis items she'd ever bought for me. As I walked toward the living room, I realized I could hear them talking even from the front hall. The egg pulsed as Lena and Ernie whispered to each other.

"I think Cass is more upset about it than I am," I heard Lena whisper, "though she'd never admit it."

It felt as if I were hearing through my head.

Ernie came out to the kitchen when he heard me come in. His hat sat uneasily on his head, and there were deep brown stains under his arms from delivering so much mail in the heat.

"She seems especially fixated today," he said. "Maybe the *Aloha* disc was a bad idea."

I shrugged. My head throbbed too much to talk about our parents, even though I knew the subject would be unavoidable.

"You look different today, Cass," he said. "Prettier somehow."

I pulled the cap down to my eyebrow line.

"Thanks, Ernie," I said, and I meant it, though I suddenly tasted lox again and thought I might burst into tears.

"Where did you get that cap?" Lena asked, as she shuffled into the living room in her open-toed sandals. I hugged her and couldn't help but look down at the missing toenail. Maybe Vance was right. It was something of a travesty, my sister's beautiful feet ruined.

"Can I try it on?"

She poured red wine into plastic stemware.

"No, hon, not just now," I said. "I've got a terrible headache, and the hat just seems to help. It was the only one I could find. You gave it to me, remember?"

She smiled at me as she reached for her glass of wine.

"I don't think you've ever worn it before," she said. "It looks good on you. Really pretty."

I smiled back and sat down at the kitchen table. I glanced down at her missing toenail and slugged some of the wine before beginning.

"So," Lena said, "this one's going to be good, isn't it?"

I sighed as Ernie opened the carton of cigarettes and lined the packs up end to end, like boxcars, on the table.

"I don't know about that," I said, patting Lena's hand. "But I do know that this one's true."

We only let Lena have a few sips of the wine because of her medication. She still got pedicures because of the threat of further fungus, always changing the color of her polish from deep reds to darker browns according to the season. Having only nine toenails, she said, did not give a woman reason to neglect her feet.

Just as having no parents, she said, was not reason enough to forget them.

I remember little about my childhood before the age of fifteen, when I "blossomed," as Ma liked to say. And why bother? If our parents found it dull enough not to let the rosy tinge of memories get to them—at least enough to make them stay on a bit longer—then why should I?

Besides, I think I knew as well as they did that there were no rosy memories. Gray ones, maybe, and some blue, but not too much in the rosy category—which is a shame, if you think about it, since I look best in warmer colors.

Lena, however, remembers everything. Or so she claims. And what she doesn't remember, we fill in by making it up. She remembers Ma wearing long braids before her hair fell out, singing to the Mamas and the Papas in the shower, painting our toenails lilac, making Santa-shaped cakes, long before I wanted to be a Jew. She remembers Our Father sitting in his recliner with his socks off, watching reruns of *Bonanza* and making us sundaes, which we all ate while we kids rooted for Little Joe, and Ma went on about Lorne Greene being the best television father she'd ever known.

All I remember, except for snippets here and there, are the trips to the zoo. And those are the ones I'd like to forget. Every time we came home Ma would whisper in the car, "I just don't understand Cass. All those beautiful tigers and leopards, and she only has eyes for the rhinos."

I'd like to know what she'd say about that now.

One of the things I do remember vividly are the stories about the first days after I was born. Ma loved to tell those stories, never seeming to tire of repeating what an unattractive baby I'd been. It seemed to give her a lot of joy, having birthed an ugly baby who became a beautiful girl.

"You sure have blossomed, Cass," she'd say, shaking her head and scratching at the bald spots at the top of her scalp, "but believe me, no one would have believed it to look at you then."

I was born with milk pimples strung like tiny white pearls across my nose, one eye squeezed shut like a pirate's, blotches of matted black hair that stood up on end and refused to settle under the knit caps they use in hospitals. When Our Father came to visit, he and Ma would pad down to the nursery and peer in at me, hoping I'd been trans-formed overnight into one of the pretty pink babies with blond fuzz or dark curls, instead of the pale purple and gray blob in the incubator.

"A little better today," Our Father would tell Ma, his hand on the knots at the back of her hospital gown.

Ma would sigh, lean her forehead against the cool glass.

"A little," she'd say. "But not much."

When I became a hair replacement specialist, I posted a sign on my work station: *Looking a little better is not enough. Always aim high.*

As we ate the wonton soup and lo mein Ernie had brought, I felt the bump pulsing in my head. Lena had stared at me through the entire story, but I'd kept my eyes on my plate and tried not to look back. Every few minutes Ernie would set down his chopsticks—he believed in being authentic—and stare off in the distance.

I could tell that Lena was disappointed in what I'd told her, but it wasn't as if we had a wealth of memories to choose from. What was there to say about people who'd been gone for eighteen years, the exact amount of time they'd been around? When they left, we were coming out into the world, and now we were in our mid-thirties with Lena terrified of the world. Still, she loved the stories, and it was my duty as a sister, I thought, to provide them.

When the meal was over, Ernie gathered up our plates and washed them in the sink while Lena sat smoking cigarettes and fretting over whether to cancel her session with the internet shrink. Staring at the screen for so many hours a day navigating through her anxiety chat rooms and e-mail had begun to strain her eyes.

"That was a very interesting story, Cass," Ernie said with his hands full of suds. His one shoulder drooped from the constant weight of his mailbag. He loved my sister, I thought, but she was too caught up in her panic to see it.

He dried his hands on a dish towel and glanced over at Lena, who was snapping the rubber band on her wrist—a sure signal that her anxiety was getting the better of her.

"Your parents must have been interesting people," he said.

I looked over at Lena and felt the egg twitching beneath my cap.

"That's just the thing, Ernie," I said, reaching beneath the rim to scratch the bump. "Without Elvis, I think they would have been pretty dull."

Lena's eyes filled with tears, and she snapped her rubber band. I reached over and snapped it several times for her.

"I just can't believe that story's true," she said, her lower lip quivering. "How could you have been so ugly? And how could they think that about you?" She got up from the chair and stood facing me, her hands gripping the back of the chair.

"That's just another story," she said. "Come on, Cass, I know when you're making things up."

I touched her hand with my fingertip and rubbed her sore wrist, which was red from all the snapping.

"I'm sorry, Lena," I said, "but that one is true."

Lena knew our parents were going to leave long before they actually left. She'd felt it, she said, the way animals sense an oncoming storm, she said. When she was twelve, she had recurring dreams of our parents holed up in a church with Elvis's face on the front, and no matter how many times she banged on the door, they refused to let her in. Later when Ma accompanied Our Father and Rusty to nearby towns for impersonator gigs, Lena was sure they wouldn't come home again.

She'd always had problems with separation, but she got worse after one day at the zoo when our parents went off to buy ice cream cones and didn't return for over two hours. We searched the lion cages, the picnic area, and the concession stand, but there was no sign of them.

When she wouldn't stop crying, I dragged her by the arm to the rhinos and leaned her up against the wall. The rhinos were just standing there, their horns raised in the air toward us.

It was then that she started to scream.

"They're gone, Cass, they're gone!" she shrieked, over and over, until a passing security guard came over and held her by the wrist.

"What seems to be the problem here, girls?" he asked.

I stared at the rhinos, who seemed to be looking at us warily, and then turned to the guard and shrugged my shoulders.

"My sister thinks our parents are lost," I said. "We just can't find them."

He handed Lena a balled-up tissue and pointed toward two figures leaning against a fence about thirty yards away.

"Those folks over there," he said, bending down toward Lena, "they wouldn't happen to be your parents, would they?"

Just then the figures ambled toward us, and Lena ran, her sneakers kicking back dust in my face. The security guard picked up the ball of tissue Lena had dropped on the ground.

"I'd say that's them," he said with a wink, "wouldn't you?"

I stayed fixed to my spot at the rhino den and let my arms dangle over the edge of the brick wall.

"Yes, that's them," I said, and as I turned to face them, I saw Lena clinging to Ma's waist while Ma just stood there with her hands at her sides.

She couldn't hug her, not then, and certainly, not now, which was all Lena really wanted.

I don't know if she remembers that day. She's never mentioned it. It's certainly not one of the stories I've ever chosen to tell her.

After dinner we sat in the living room together, Lena and I on one side of the couch, Ernie in Our Father's old recliner. Lena slipped in the *Aloha from Hawaii* DVD, skipping the theme music from *2001* and letting Elvis launch into "See See Rider," his leg shaking in the white jumpsuit, his name in red flashing letters behind him in different languages. Lena sighed as the applause rang out, and propped her bare foot on my lap.

"You know, when they first left, I could still feel them, just like I did with my toenail when Vance took it off," she said wistfully, as the guitarist played the opening riffs of "Burning Love." "Every night I'd look down at it, and expect it to come back."

"When I watch Elvis, I feel just like that," she said.

She snapped her rubber band. I massaged her heel and felt my head throb.

"Like what?" Ernie asked. "Like Elvis isn't dead, or that you miss your parents?"

I cut in before Lena could answer. I was intrigued by the phantom feeling of the missing toenail and wanted to avoid the subject of our parents whenever possible—which was hardly ever possible to do.

"I don't think I've ever thought of my toenail as something I could feel," I said, glancing over at Lena, whose face was growing more flushed by the minute. "I mean, I'm not sure I'd know the difference between one toenail or another if I lost one."

Her heel felt warm in my hand.

"Would I be able to say, 'That's my big toenail missing there, the leader,' as opposed to, 'Nope, it's my pinky toenail that's gone now?'"

Lena sighed and pressed her head against the back of the sofa.

"Exactly," she said. "That's exactly what I mean."

That night, for the first time since our parents left, we did not mention them at all for the rest of the night, not even during the King's camp rendition of "Fever"—Our Father's favorite—with Elvis wiggling a leg to the drums or shaking his shoulders, laughing to himself as the women screamed. We watched the concert all the way to the end, after Elvis threw his eagle-spangled cape out into the audience, staring at the television even after the screen turned blue.

SEVEN

You must understand this: I've never blamed Elvis. Not before the horn, and certainly not after. What our parents did with— or in the name of—Elvis was their own doing, not his. Elvis didn't force them into the night.

What I learned about Our Father after he left far exceeded what little I knew of him all those years he'd reclined in his La-Z-Boy and listened to Elvis records. I learned that he'd memorized every line of dialogue to the film *Viva Las Vegas*, and that he was relieved that Elvis had married "Cilla," as Our Father invariably called her, and not Ann-Margret. He considered marrying Cilla the smartest move the King had ever made, especially since she'd done a wonderful job raising Lisa Marie. I learned that Our Father sometimes called Ma "Sattnin," Elvis's nickname for his mother—and later, "Cilla"—when he and Ma made love, a fact I could have done without knowing—and that he knew the names of every member of the Memphis Mafia. Of course I knew he loved the scarf-bearing Charlie Hodge. I also learned that Our Father had been one of the first people to tear out pages of the bodyguards' tell-all book when it hit stores just before the King collapsed on his porcelain throne.

Sometimes I'm not sure how I know these things about him. Some of them Lena has told me, and some of them we may have pieced together.

But after all the time they've been gone, it's difficult to decipher what's true about our parents and what we've made up.

I've come to think, finally, that it doesn't matter. It's what we believe that counts.

Later, after Ernie had gone, I stood over Lena's shoulder as she talked to the internet shrink. At first she'd wanted to call herself "Aggie" for her agoraphobia, but the name had been taken, so she chose "Homebound" instead.

HOMEBOUND: *Cass was an ugly baby.*

PSYKING: *Elvis was a surviving twin.*

HOMEBOUND: *She says Ma told her this all the time. And that she had milk pimples. And that she had hair that stuck up all over the place.*

PSYKING: *Many babies have unruly hair. I'm not sure it's known whether in fact Elvis had hair as an infant. Certainly not enough for a pompadour, I'm sure.*

HOMEBOUND: *We watched the Aloha movie tonight, all the way through. Ernie gave it to me for my birthday.*

PSYKING: *Happy Birthday. That was the last time Elvis looked well.*

HOMEBOUND: *It was a beautiful jumpsuit. But it pains me to watch it.*

PSYKING: *Of course it does. It's hard to see someone so vital having ended up the way he did. I've always thought that should have been his farewell concert.*

HOMEBOUND: *I kept looking at my toenail and thinking about our parents. It was so hard to concentrate. Just awful.*

PSYKING: *He had such thick sideburns then. Down to his chin. And those cheekbones . . .*

HOMEBOUND: *Cass is here. She has something wrong with her head.*

PSYKING: *"Don't Cry, Daddy" has always been one of my favorite songs. I've never found an ounce of* schmaltz *in that one, no matter what anyone says.*

HOMEBOUND: *I'm feeling faint.*

PSYKING: *Take deep breaths. You know, Lena, you should pay special attention to* Blue Hawaii. *I think it would speak to you. Especially when the Hawaiian woman does the hula dance in the upper right-hand corner and the waves come tumbling in.*

HOMEBOUND: *My heart's pounding now. Hard.*

PSYKING: *It will pass. Think about Elvis. That always helps. They have that jumpsuit on display at Graceland. You should see it when you're well. Make it a long-term goal.*

HOMEBOUND: *Cass is taking off her cap.*

PSYKING: *Stay focused. Now, tell me: what is your favorite Elvis song?*

HOMEBOUND: *What is that thing?*

PSYKING: *I don't know that one. "You Gave Me a Mountain" is mine.*

HOMEBOUND: *Cass has a bump on her head. It's huge. I feel sick.*

PSYKING: *This time, Lord, he gave you a mountain, Lena.*

HOMEBOUND: *Can I take another Xanax?*

PSYKING: *A mountain you may never climb . . .*

74

When Lena fell off the chair, I helped her up and ran for a washcloth for her head.

PSYKING: *Elvis took Xanax. And Dilaudid, and Percodan, barbiturates, any number of depressants. I read the autopsy report online. It's quite fascinating, even what some people believe is the misspelling of his name on his tombstone.*

Before she could stop me, I sat in her computer chair and typed in a message:

HOMEBOUND: *What the hell does any of this have to do with Elvis??*
PSYKING: *You're resisting again, Lena. Remember what I've said about resistance.*
HOMEBOUND: *What's that, you quack?*

There was a long pause while I waited for his response.

PSYKING: *Elvis is everywhere.*

And then he signed off.

When she was well enough to stand, I helped Lena to her bed and pressed the washcloth to the back of her neck. The egg on my head beat in time with my racing heart.

"Jesus, Lena, you never told me he was an Elvis freak," I said, as calmly as I could manage. "I thought he was a decent shrink."

She covered her eyes with the washcloth.

"Don't be so naive, Cass," she said. "The world's full of Elvis freaks."

I didn't say anything until she peered at me through a space in the washcloth at the bump on my head.

"You're in worse shape than I am."

"Thanks," I said, and then we got up together without saying a word, joining hands with our arms crossed at the wrists. We started spinning just like we did when we were kids, slowly at first, then faster and faster until the room became a wild blur. We'd spin whenever we got back from the zoo, and Ma would lead Our Father up the stairs by the hand, locking them in their bedroom for hours, as if they'd never come out. Over and over we whirled around, until we both fell back on the bed and lay there with the room spinning as we fought to catch our breath.

Lena suffered panic attacks for years, but she stopped going outside completely when she was twenty-eight, after she dyed her hair black, after Boyd had left her. Joan had made a "Cheer Up Lena" dinner as a consolation. Joan had never thought much of Boyd, who wore a gray ponytail that Joan swore was meant as a deliberate mockery of male pattern baldness and not just an attempt to look as if his hair wasn't desperately receding. I'd never liked Boyd much either, though he did bring my sister four brief years of happiness before running off with a dental hygienist.

Boyd had a nasal midwestern accent and spent the first year of their marriage trying to convince Lena that Elvis lay in a vegetative state at Graceland, which was the reason no visitors were permitted upstairs. Boyd played guitar and decried the injustice of Lena being named after Lena Horne, who he swore was a Caucasian woman masquerading as a light-skinned black woman, in Boyd's words, "just for attention." He thought our parents were cowards for "cutting out the way they did," as he liked to put it, and though Lena tried to keep him from saying so, I was sure part of her agreed with him.

"Well, one good thing about Boyd's being gone," Joan whispered while we waited for Lena to join us at the table, "is that we don't have to look at that damned ponytail of his anymore."

Boyd and Lena got married on a June day in the backyard. He wore a leather vest and Lena wore a white gauze dress that showed her panties in the sunlight. I'd moved out as soon as Boyd had moved in, and because of the cost of the move and the fact that Boyd was perpetually out of work, we didn't have money for extras, like a white tent or the pink balloons she'd wanted. I'd spent half the day trying to coax her into the shade, but she was so happy to have met someone who finally understood her that she kept pushing me away and telling me to leave her alone.

"I want to feel the sun on me," she said. "It's my wedding day, and Boyd likes to see me in the sun."

"But people can see your underwear," I said. She spent the rest of the day under the tree in the backyard.

After three years of marriage, Boyd hacked off his ponytail in the bathroom one day and said he'd met a woman at the dentist's office named Diana and that it was time for him to move on.

"Diana, as in the Supremes?" Joan had asked, as Lena cried and cried.

After that "cheer-up" dinner, Lena couldn't move beyond the front door. Boyd had been gone a month by then, declaring to her just before leaving that he'd had his teeth cleaned "and a whole lot more." Even though I knew she was depressed and that her attacks were getting worse, we still managed to have lunch at a café while Lena stared at her wedding snapshots and ate scones with butter. We laughed at a man in the corner who hummed "Can't Help Falling in Love" while sipping at his tea. Stupidly I thought this meant she was going to be O.K.

When she finally came out of the bathroom that night with her hair dyed black, Joan and I dropped our forks and stared at her. She held her arms out at her sides and twirled around. Blotches of black dye stained the back of her neck.

"Lena, honey, what on earth have you done?" Joan shrieked.

I was speechless at first, thinking about Ma and all her bad dye jobs, trying to cover her baldness but only making it more pronounced.

Lena stared at me with this loopy grin, and I said the first thing that came into my head.

"I think the King would have been proud," I said.

Joan glared at me, but Lena smiled and ate everything Joan passed to her without another word.

The next day Lena didn't show up for lunch, and when I called to find out what had happened, she said she could no longer go outside.

"It's just not safe," she said. "I'll never be safe again."

At first I tried everything to get her to come out. I hired a behavioral therapist who prescribed everything from desensitization to making Lena write down every negative thought she ever had. There were notebooks full of them that she later kept under her bed. I sent Rose to the house to give her pedicures and tried to lure her out to the front stoop to let her toes dry in the sun, but every time she neared the front door, she'd hold onto the walls, then run back to her bedroom and cry out that she was dying. Even Joan tried to help, buying her Lena

Horne records and leaving them on the front lawn as incentive, but nothing worked. Eventually we gave up.

I should have seen it coming. Boyd had. A few times Lena had canceled lunch dates or refused to go out at night. Boyd had said from the beginning that we were wasting our time.

"Leave her be," he'd say on his way out at night when I'd come over to assure her she wasn't having a heart attack, that her mind would not disappear. "She's a shut-in now. Some people are born to be shut-ins, and Lena's one of them."

Even though I tried to explain that the proper word for her condition was "agoraphobia," that it trivialized her problems to call her a "shut-in," and had even brought him pamphlets from the doctor's office, Boyd never used any other word to describe her condition. To him she was a shut-in and no other word would suffice.

Secretly I've always thought our parents had suspected this would happen and that if they ever did return, they'd feel vindicated by Lena's agoraphobia. Except for concert tours and rides on his golf carts around Graceland, in his last years, Elvis had been something of a shut-in, too.

Ernie started visiting her in the afternoons and talked to her through the mail slot, though she wouldn't allow him to come inside, not at first. I never knew what they talked about on those afternoons, but one day, Lena locked herself in her bedroom and wouldn't answer the phone or speak to Ernie or Joan or me, no matter how many times we banged at the door or called. When I finally threatened to summon the police, she came to the door in her bathrobe and slippers and stared past me, as if I weren't there.

"Boyd's gone," she said, her forehead blackened by hair dye that she hadn't washed away. "And Elvis is dead. I just don't want to live anymore."

Though she's since denied ever having said this, I can still see the look on her face as she stood there that day in her rumpled bathrobe, moving away from the door as I came inside. Sunlight flooded the room as I stepped forward to wrap my arms around her, but she shielded her eyes and backed into the darkened room.

EIGHT

If Joan hadn't come for me, I would never have bothered going to the dermatologist. Between the cat's constant jumping on my head and the neighbors' headboard banging against the wall all night, I hadn't slept more than an hour. They were newlyweds, and they lived on the other side of the duplex I rented. Normally I pulled a pillow over my head to drown out their moans, but even the pillow hadn't helped with Griz raking at it with her claws and the sense that their lovemaking had snaked its way inside my head. When Joan came to the door, I didn't even bother to put on my "T.C.B." hat.

"Good God, look at you," she said, flipping her hair over one shoulder as Griz stuck her tail in the air and pressed her behind into Joan's leg. I kicked the cat with my bare foot and took the lattes Joan had brought. "That thing looks worse than it did yesterday."

I nodded and sat down at the kitchen table. As I wrapped my hand around the cup, the feel of styrofoam was so intense that I had to pull my hand away. I could hear the honeymooners sighing through the wall.

"I couldn't sleep with that racket," I said, standing up to pound my fist against the wall. "Those two have been at it all night."

Joan sipped her latte and pressed her ear to the wall.

"I don't hear anything," she said.

The moans escalated, the woman panting as if she were being strangled.

"You don't hear that?" I asked, banging on the wall again. "It's driving me nuts."

She paused, tilting her head toward the wall to listen.

"No," she shrugged. "I don't hear a thing."

Griz sat lapping herself with her legs spread, long thick swipes with her sandpaper tongue. Joan eyed me suspiciously and took a long sip. Wafts of sex clung to the air.

"You let that toe-hacker look at it, didn't you?" she asked. "I knew you would."

I shook my head and pressed at the egg. I could feel it throbbing under my fingertips.

"No," I said, remembering the feel of Vance's erection pressed against my hip and the smell of his chemicals in my hair. "I swear."

We finished our lattes in silence. I picked up the styrofoam cups and paused a minute before throwing them in the trash. With my thumb and forefinger, I circled the rim of the cups, mentally comparing the feel of the styrofoam with the hardness of the bump on my head.

At Joan's insistence, I tied a blue scarf around my head and put on an old sweatshirt from Regal's that Maureen had made for Christmas one year. I didn't even notice the Santa Claus dancing in the corner with a white wig in his hand until we were halfway to the dermatologist's office—though it was clearly out of place on that sunny June day.

"Jesus Christ," I said, holding the sweatshirt out from my body as we stopped at a red light. "This is something Lena would do."

Lena was famous for wearing Cupid earrings long after Valentine's Day and putting up her Christmas tree in May to feel "festive," she said. Since she never left the house, no one tried to dissuade her. I'd agreed to allow for some eccentricities because of her agoraphobia and Boyd's abandonment, and Ernie said he liked seeing the wreaths in her windows on the Fourth of July.

"At least she has a mind of her own," Ernie told me one day as I was climbing the porch steps, and who could argue with that?

But I had a life. I would have masses of people at my funeral—Lena had said so.

When we pulled into the parking lot of the dermatologist's office, Joan reached in her purse for a joint and passed it to me.

"It breaks my heart to say this to you, Cass," she said, as I sucked in the first breath of smoke and held it, "but if that bump on your head keeps growing, that Santa Claus sweatshirt will suit you to a T."

Once you've grown a horn, you learn quickly who your friends are.

You may find that the ones who seem to know you best know you hardly at all.

But who can know anyone, really, especially someone with a horn on her head?

The dermatologist, Dr. Javits, was a middle-aged Jewish man with dusty tchotchkes inside a glass case—thimbles, little porcelain dolls, painted seashells. His wife had come to the spa once for a consultation when her hair became dangerously thin during menopause. Joan had told me she'd spent forty minutes after the computer imaging explaining that hair addition would be painless, but the woman had started crying and said she couldn't bear the thought of all those little clips stuck to her head. She was sure they'd penetrate her brain. I didn't tell him this, though—what husband wants to think of his wife's baldness, let alone what needs to be done to cover it?—but I did brag that I could recite the beginnings of the Seder from memory. He looked puzzled but smiled afterwards, as if bestowing on me the honor of being a good Jew, then asked if I had any allergies to medications or food that I knew of.

"Ham," I lied. "I could never eat ham."

He smiled to himself and wrote notes in my folder.

"Just as well," he said, scratching at the bald spot on the back of his head. "The fat content in ham is very high, not good for the skin."

I liked him right away. I even made a personal vow to do his wife's image consult myself if she ever came back to the spa.

His nurse handed me a cotton gown and glanced at the Santa Claus sweatshirt as she showed me how to tie it in the back.

"I was feeling festive," I said with a laugh as I took the gown from her.

She smiled and said nothing as she closed the door behind her. I glanced over at the *mezuzah* hanging above his office door and felt a deep blush spread over my cheeks. His *mezuzah* hung high on the right side of the door. I was sure my own was too low and worried that I may have even hung it on the left side. I wanted to know what the Hebrew words meant, but I was too ashamed to ask.

By the time Dr. Javits tapped at the door, I'd rolled my sweatshirt and jeans into a ball on the chair and tied the gown in double knots at my neck and waist. The back of the scarf tickled the bare part of my back as I turned to face him.

"Now, where is this bump you've been describing?" he asked. "On the back of your neck or beneath your breasts?"

He moved to untie the knots at my nape when I didn't answer. I felt at the scarf and realized that I'd never bothered to tell him where the egg lurked.

"No," I said, feeling his cold fingers on my back as he began to untie me. I took a deep breath, pulled the scarf away, and lowered my head.

"It's here," I whispered, letting my hair fall like a curtain around my face.

I watched as he stepped to the front of the table and lifted my hair at the sides, then cupped my chin in his hands.

I thought of Ma with fistfuls of hair in her hands, Cousin It/Crystal preparing herself for another day at the hospital for the *meshuge* people.

"Ahh, yes, there it is," he said, pushing my bangs back with his thumbs and prodding the egg with his fingers. He breathed through his nose and held his thumb across it to measure its size, then made notations on his clipboard.

He turned back to me and pressed down on the bump with both thumbs, hard. It didn't hurt, but a crunching sound filled the room.

"How odd," he said. "No fluid there. In fact, it feels a bit like plastic."

He washed his hands at the sink and put on his glasses.

"More like styrofoam," I said. "At least that's how it felt at first."

He nodded and turned to write something on his notepad.

"Yes," he said. "Quite like styrofoam, I'd say, only harder. More resistant."

I took a deep breath and let it out in a rush.

"But it's not styrofoam, is it?" I asked.

He turned back to me and lifted a razor-like instrument to my head.

"No, I don't think so," he said. "Highly unlikely."

He scraped at the bump with his razor, bits of pink flesh gathering on the sharp silvery end. I felt no pain, just the vague sensation of being pressed upon, prodded.

"Have you ever seen anything like it?" I asked when he was finished and had labeled the scraping with my name and sealed it into a plastic bag. I lowered my eyes and stared down at the tips of my fingernails, which had chipped at the edges from picking at the bump on my head.

He pressed a compress to the bump although there had been no blood.

"Not quite like it, no," he said. "But I wouldn't worry at this point." He patted my knee and closed the file with my information in it. "I'm going to prescribe some antibiotics and ointment. More than likely these things are fungal, or the beginnings of a cyst, though they can appear rather nasty. I'll send the scraping out to the lab. Usually the ointment and antibiotics take several days to have an effect, and I'm sure you'll be back to your pretty self in no time." He smiled again and patted my arm. "No need to worry."

I tried to smile at his comment, though he confirmed my worst suspicions: I was hideous.

"In the meantime," he said, shaking my hand and giving me a conspiratory wink, "stay away from ham."

As he turned to leave, I felt the effects of the pot rush over me. I wondered if he'd noticed that I was stoned. For a minute I had the urge to yell after him that I would never eat ham, that I'd been named after Mama Cass and had spent half my life afraid of choking, that I could have been named Elvis and saved myself a world of trouble. But as soon as the door closed behind him, I felt myself relax again, the bump pulsing rhythmically in my head as if to music only it could hear.

A rhinoceros horn grows at a rate of roughly three inches a year. Mine took one week.

This became my daily routine, which I pasted to my bathroom wall:

7 a.m.: Awaken to find cat sleeping on my head, tail curled over my forehead and dander up my nose.

7:15: Stumble to mirror in bathroom, flip on light switch, and stare at egg until spots form in my eyes, concentric circles with orange rims, moving in closer until they seem to wind their way into my head. Splash water on my face and begin scrubbing the egg with sea salts.

7:30: Apply astringent and toner to oily area surrounding egg, down tip of nose, and across chin. Repeat if cotton swab test reveals oil still lingering at sides of egg.

7:45: Stare in mirror. Squeeze at egg with fingers, despite warnings from Dr. Javits. Wash hands thoroughly. Repeat.

8:00: Apply fungal ointment to egg and surrounding area. Wait for cream to absorb. Pour full glass of water and take two pills prescribed by Javits.

8:10: Feed cat. Return to mirror for more staring.

8:25: Bang on wall to stop honeymooners from screwing. Light candles to drown out coital smell.

8:30: Begin makeup application—base, foundation, powder, careful not to smear ointment on egg. Do not corrode egg with makeup, as it seems to resist being colored. Apply baby powder to egg to stifle tingling sensations. Smooth on lilac eye shadow and brown eyeliner, heavy, to draw attention to eyes and away from egg. Smudge eyeliner at corners. Brush and pencil eyebrows. Use mascara wand to apply mascara; dry with hair dryer.

9:00: Sing bars of "I Feel Pretty" until throbbing of egg subsides.

Joan stalled Maureen long enough for me to fill the prescriptions and change into a denim minidress to match my blue scarf. I took a long time applying my makeup, using a darker beige for the bump and a paler shade for the rest of my face. I smothered it in pressed powder and brushed my cheeks and nose with soft pink blush. With my lips lined and heavy mascara on my eyes, the scarf looked almost fashionable. We often sold scarves to women undergoing chemotherapy, and I hoped the one I chose would set my clients at ease.

"Vance called," the receptionist announced on my way in the door. "He's canceled all his bunion patients and said he's desperate to see you."

I took the piece of paper with the message on it. She'd underlined the word "desperate" three times in red ink.

"The emphasis is his, not mine," she said, buffing her nails and blowing on them. "Oh, and by the way," she added as I headed to the back room, "nice scarf."

When I checked the day's roster, I noticed that Ellen Graham had booked a two-hour session. Though we weren't close in recent years, she'd been a great help to Lena after our parents had left and had even gotten Lena the job as a postal clerk because she knew how integral the mail had become in Lena's life. I'd known Ellen since high school when a kid in driver's ed had exploded a car battery during class. The kid who'd done it was the son of a mechanic in town and had failed his permit test three times because he couldn't distinguish between yield and stop signs. The battery acid splashed the sides of Ellen's face and had burned off most of her hair, which had never properly grown back. Scarred lines fell down her face like teardrops.

She'd become a client of mine after a botched transplant. I'd sold her various additions that she could interchange and attach at home, but whenever she needed a lift, she'd come in to the spa.

"Your client is waiting," Maureen said, as I located Ellen's card in her file. I nodded but didn't look up, jotting notes.

"Oh, Cass," Maureen said, "I always knew you had the kind of empathy we need in a place like this." She fingered the edges of my scarf and smiled. "You can't even imagine what seeing a beautiful woman like you will do to lift the spirits of some of the women having chemo or those who have been burned, like your poor friend Ellen."

I forced a smile and felt the bump pulsate.

"Your beauty is inspiring, Cass," she said. "It takes a special woman, not only to look the way you do, but to feel for the rest of us, too."

But I felt little that day, either for the clients or for myself. All I could feel was the bump.

At my station I sorted out the clips and hair pieces I thought Ellen might like. Her scars looked especially deep, with shadows around the edges as if she'd brushed the scars with mascara.

"I've been crying," she said, as I began to ease away the clips holding her hair additions in place, "in case you couldn't tell."

"Oh?" I said, continuing to remove the clips and turning her chair so she wouldn't have to face the mirror.

"One of the kids broke a double-A battery this morning, and it just brought it all back to me," she said in a rush. "J.R., my youngest boy, the one with all the curly hair, spilled battery acid on his fingers trying to get his remote control car to work. He wasn't hurt or anything, thank God, but it just set me off."

I suggested she close her eyes while I removed the hair additions from the sides and top of her head.

"I don't think about it much anymore, but sometimes it's just like it happened yesterday." She kept her eyes closed as I lifted the new pieces gingerly with my fingertips.

"I guess I don't have to tell you what that's like, Cass," she said. "Even after all this time, there mustn't be a day that goes by that you don't wonder where your parents went." She opened her eyes and looked at me. "How many years has it been now?" she asked.

I cleared my throat.

"Eighteen," I said, "but who's counting?"

Neither of us laughed.

Over the years, Ellen had taken great pains to bring Lena any information she could find about Elvis. She left them on the front porch—rare recordings, postcards, articles about Priscilla. Her father had been a huge fan of Frank Sinatra, and

Ellen had even named one of her sons in his honor: Francis Albert. When her father died listening to "Summer Wind," Ellen called us first. If anyone could understand what being a fan was like, Lena and I could, she said.

"Do you think you'll ever find them?" she asked.

I stopped to tie my scarf into a double knot in the back.

I wanted to say that I'd long since given up looking, and that our parents' obsession with Elvis had offered few clues, that they'd left only bits of memorabilia in their wake. Wherever her father had gone, he'd taken his love of Sinatra *with* him. Our parents had left Elvis behind, to be pored over, sifted through, dissected.

"Doubtful," I said, and stopped to wash my hands at the sink. "But you know Lena. She never gives up."

Ellen gave me a sad smile and tilted her head back as I went to work pinning the additions to what remained of her hair. The best way to deflect attention from the scars, I always told her, was to accentuate her better features. She had a strong jaw and pouty lips, which was why I always gave her heavy bangs and softly curled sides that brushed against her cheekbones. I wondered if the same techniques would work with the bump, but at least Ellen's scars were small and her hair loss could be covered up. If the bump kept growing, I thought, *nothing* would deflect attention from it, *nothing* would keep it hidden, even with all my training.

When I was finished, Ellen smiled at herself in the mirror and pressed her lips together.

"Tell Lena I have some new Elvis stuff for her—just some trinkets I found at a tag sale," she said, stuffing the tip in the pocket of my smock. "And I really love your scarf. It's a new look for you. You look different with it on, even prettier than usual."

I thanked her and watched as she settled her bill at the desk. I thought of how she looked that day in driver's ed as the acid seared her skin and hair. It was important that I'd been there to bear witness to what had changed Ellen, I thought, even though I didn't feel brave enough to show her what was happening to me. At least she knew what had caused her scars, I thought, feeling the beads of sweat pooling in the folds of the scarf. Three days had gone by, and I still had no idea what had brought about the eruption in my head, though I noticed that I suddenly had an overwhelming craving for ham on rye.

NINE

Elvis's spiritual adviser was also his hairdresser. When he came to style Elvis's hair, Larry Geller, the hairdresser-cum-Dalai Lama, would educate the King on the ins and outs of Eastern philosophy. He had even, I'm told, introduced Elvis to the Talmud.

Now there, I've always wanted to tell Ma, was a piece of Elvis trivia you could choke on.

Joan and I finished a joint before I left for the day. The prescription Javits had given me said nothing about mixing it with marijuana, and as far as I could tell from the few times I'd snuck into the ladies' room to check on the bump, nothing had changed. After the battery acid incident, I wondered if Ellen tried to look at herself in the mirror and imagine she were back to normal, her skin clear and unmarked, her scalp unsinged. If I were Ellen, I'd have left the headlights on every night and killed the battery over and over again in revenge. Elvis would have shot the hood full of holes, and his bodyguards would have laughed. Maybe I'd suggest both of these ideas to Ellen the next time she came in, I thought, taking a long hit from the joint.

And I'd keep my kids away from batteries altogether.

Joan pinched the last of the joint with a hair clip and sucked in a mouthful of smoke.

"The toe-hacker called again, you know," she said, spraying the air in the room with a spritz gel we ordered specially to mask the tobacco smell in the hair of heavy smokers.

"You're going to have to let him look at your head. He's not going to take no for an answer."

I popped a breath mint in my mouth and then brushed my lips with clear gloss for added shine. Vance and I hadn't had sex in over a week, since I'd had my period and he'd been bombarded with bunion patients.

Though I cringe now at making such a bad pun—the truth was, I was horny as hell.

"You know," Joan continued, slipping off her white jacket and hanging it on one of the hooks on the wall behind us, "I think this thing on your head is all tied in with that toe-hacker. I mean, how can you keep dating a man who practically amputated your sister's toe? That's got to come out somehow. I know you haven't had much luck with men, Cass, but if Lena had one thing going for her, it was those pretty feet, and he went and took that away."

I've often thought that Joan had more invested in Lena's feet than Lena herself. On the day of Lena's procedure, we had to give Joan as many Xanax as Lena had. Joan had hammer toes as a kid and hated podiatrists. Lena had no idea how beautiful her feet had been, Joan always said after the surgery. With me for a sister, it couldn't have been easy for Lena to watch men staring at me wherever I went. The one beautiful thing that was hers alone was her feet, and Vance had taken it from her, Joan said, ripped it away, just like so much of Lena's life.

"She had fungus so bad that it bordered on gangrene," I said, wrinkling my nose to emphasize the distaste I felt at the thought of Lena's diseased toenail. "It was either the toenail went or the whole toe itself could have gone, and my sister had enough sense to let go of the toenail."

I thought of Vance's guilt at having detoenailed my sister. Since then, he spent nearly all his free time working in his lab trying to find a way to produce keratin, the stuff that hair and nails are made of. Once, during sex, he told me that he believed he'd come close to finding a solution, but when I pressed him for details, he slipped on his pants and said, "One should never talk about feet at a time like this." I never asked him about his lab again.

Joan and I said good-bye in the parking lot. I tightened the scarf around my head and took a deep breath. Blood thumped through my forehead and burned my cheeks.

"You'd just better hope Vance doesn't get any ideas when he sees that bump of yours," Joan said on the way to her car. "He might want to hack that off, too."

If I'd known what was coming, I might have said something in response, but as I hurried across the parking lot, I swore I could hear Elvis's signature theme from *2001* playing in the distance, ready to make his entrance. I jammed the key into the ignition and revved the engine. A white leather-clad leg shook in my mind's eye, the kettle drums thundering in my head.

Vance was waiting for me in the shadows in front of my house. The honeymoon couple's car was gone, and the bulb that lit the walkway and my side of the house had burnt out. I knew it was Vance by the slope of his shoulders and the glow of his teeth when he smiled—he'd recently had them bleached, a week-long process that had left his breath smelling vaguely medicinal, his tongue tasting metallic. I found it odd for him to have reached the house before I did. Vance hated to be kept waiting and would have clipped a paraplegic's toenails or lasered some corns if he'd known I'd be running late. He kept toenail clippings—like Lena had with our parents' things—in hermetically sealed jars.

"Specimens," he called them, though what he meant by that, I was never quite sure.

He was on me as soon as I approached, the keys rattling in my hand as I struggled to open the door. With his hands on my hips, he rubbed against me from behind, his lips sucking at the back of my neck, under the silky threads dangling from the back of the scarf.

"Wait, wait," I breathed, finally throwing open the wooden door and then reaching for the latch on the screen door behind it.

"Oh, my God!" I shrieked at the sight of Griz hanging on the screen, claws curving through the tiny holes. Her ears flattened, and her mouth opened as she howled.

Vance pushed the door open, the hinges rattling as it slammed. The thud of Griz's body hitting the wall echoed through the room. She hissed and ran for the bedroom where she burrowed under the bedspread, her body sliding around, moving lumps in the bed. We stood apart from each other, breathless. Vance ripped open my blouse, unhooked my bra, and threw it across the room. I yanked at his zipper as we stumbled toward the bed. Griz screamed as I landed on top of her.

"Oh, no," I panted, "let me see about the cat," but he wouldn't listen. He parted my legs with his knee and thrust into me so fast I couldn't catch my breath.

"Fuck that cat," he said. "Tonight I'm a hound dog," he snarled in my ear.

The whole bed shook as he pounded against me, my back arching into the bed, hands tangled in his gelled hair. We moaned and writhed like never before, our bodies dripping with sweat. I could feel him peaking just as the phone rang, sliding into me with the rhythm of the phone's pulsing tones. Once, twice, three, four times, and then my own voice announcing I wasn't home.

I gripped his buttocks and held on, digging my nails in, as Lena's voice crackled through the answering machine.

"Cass," she said. "Pick up the phone! Are you there, Cass? Are you there?"

She called my name over and over, her voice growing hoarse. My whole head started to pulsate, and I felt the knots in my scarf digging at the back of my head. I twisted and turned to free myself, and as the scarf slipped back onto the pillow, Vance lifted himself higher above me and let out an anguished moan, his back tensing.

The room became a spinning whirl of colors—greens, indigos, violent blues—until I couldn't see anymore, until there was nothing but blackness and my own scream trapped inside my throat.

When I opened my eyes, I found Vance lying beside me with his hair standing up straight as a fright wig. I stumbled to the mirror and stared at myself, naked, at the thatch of pubic hair and rosy tips of my breasts, and finally—finally—having the courage to let my eyes focus on the center of my forehead, I saw what I'd suspected all along.

It was getting bigger.

All roads lead to Elvis.

I say this because Lena believes it was not our parents' departure that brought about the end of our family life, but

Elvis's. Everything that happened to us, she insisted, was all because of the King.

And yet, even if he were to blame, she still loved him.

Vance began doing an Elvis impression—which is one thing, but doing it naked, I thought, bordered on blasphemy. The sight of Vance parading around the room repulsed me, his dancing, his gangly white body, the way he sang that he was so lonesome he could die. I batted him away with a towel, but he kept on, shaking his leg, testicles bouncing.

When I first met Vance, after having been referred to him because of a particularly stubborn plantar's wart—Joan had been the one to recommend him after he'd argued against surgical straightening of her hammer toes—he did several Elvis impressions to try to woo me. But since I had such a complicated relationship with the King, I told him not to waste his time. I admit this had been something of a mistake; he'd never been able to last more than five minutes since those first few times when he'd sung "All Shook Up" as an aphrodisiac.

"All right," I said, reaching for my scarf and tying it at the back of my head while he chased me naked through the apartment, "enough is enough."

I fingered the bump on my head and then ran for a broom in the kitchen to hold him back.

"Jesus, Vance, get a grip," I said, wielding the broom as he reached out to try to grab at my scarf. "You've had enough fun for one night."

He lunged for me as I poked him with the broom handle, but he pushed it away and grabbed my head. He rubbed his face back and forth against the scarf and moaned. I fought to keep hold of the broom handle. He kept on nuzzling the scarf and hummed the guitar riffs to "Heartbreak Hotel."

The cat ran in from the bedroom and leapt at his groin. I swatted at her with the broom. Vance stumbled forward and landed with all his weight on my foot.

My scream seemed to break him out of his trance.

He looked down at the deep scratches in his groin and cupped his hands over his crotch. I fell down on the floor, gripping my foot with both hands, rocking back and forth. He kneeled down beside me and reached out to touch the heel of my foot.

"Let me see it," he begged, but I shook my head and held my hands over my ears. Everything had become unbearably loud. I could hear Griz panting.

He ran a finger over my toenails, a tear forming in the corner of his eye. A dull blue bruise had already begun to form near my big toe.

"Oh, look what I've done to your poor little sooties," he said, using Elvis's pet name for feet. When Vance and I first started dating, he asked to touch my "sooties," and it wasn't until I conferred with Lena that I found out he'd meant feet instead of breasts.

"It's all right," I said. "My sooties are fine," then added, "Just get the fuck out." It was harsh, but I just couldn't help myself.

My head felt so heavy I thought my neck would snap. Back in bed, I pulled the blankets up to my chest and kept the broom in one hand in case he came at me again. But his Elvis possession seemed to have passed. He dressed sheepishly in the corner, his back turned as he pulled on his pants. He combed his hair flat against his head.

"Cass," he said softly, coming to sit beside me, "please let me have a look at your head."

I was too weak to stop him. If I'd known how much it would cost me every time someone touched it, I never would have let him.

He pulled back the scarf and moved his fingers over the bump, down along the base and up to what had become the beginnings of the tip. I rolled my eyes up into my head to try to see what he was doing, but all I could feel was a surge of energy drain through my head and out into his hands. I tried to turn away, but he pressed his fingers deeply over the bump and made low sounds in his throat.

"Sattnin," he said. "Oh, Sattnin," and then I slapped his hand away.

"Get out, you *shmuck*, get out!" I shouted.

Vance grabbed his jacket and moved toward the door. I could feel the shame coursing through the room and heard the rapid beat of his heart as he stammered an apology, how he didn't know what had come over him, what had made him act that way.

"It was the first time I haven't thought of feet in ages," he said. "You don't know what it's like to smell feet all the time, even when you're making love."

I glared at him from the bed, my knees trembling.

"You're right," I said. "One never knows."

A dictionary of "Elvispeak":

Iddy-cream: ice cream.

Burnt: seal of approval for Elvis's well-done hamburgers, as in "Man, that's burnt!"

Dodger: pet name of Elvis's grandmother, Minnie Mae Presley.

Nungin: Cilla's nickname for Elvis, believed to be a slurred version of "young one."

Attacks: code name for sleeping pills Elvis had delivered to his bedroom at night.

I drove to Lena's as soon as I felt steady again. She called three times while I lay prostrate on the bed with Griz sleeping on my face. Whenever I tried to move her, she hissed crazily, jumping back onto my head as if terrified. Though it was difficult to breathe, her purrs resounding through my head brought me a calmness I hadn't felt since first noticing the bump—or what had then been merely a blemish—just a few short days before.

I trapped Griz in an old pillowcase—a cruel act, I admit, though at the time I couldn't find the carrier and she was in too much of a state to be allowed free reign in the car—and pressed a small packet of ice to the egg on my head before heading for Lena's house. All the lights were on when I pulled into the driveway, though it was nearly three a.m. She'd fastened Easter Bunny stickers to the inside of her front windows, a fact that would please Ernie, I thought, as I climbed the steps and opened the door, Griz in the pillowcase slung over my shoulder.

"I was worried sick," Lena said, taking the pillowcase from me and dumping Griz on the floor. "Why didn't you pick up the phone?"

I thought the cat would be a good companion for her and had often urged her to get one for herself. She'd wanted a dog for some time to keep her company when she tired of the agoraphobics' chat rooms and her internet shrink signed off, though she was afraid a dog would bark at Ernie because he carried his mailbag even during off hours.

"It was that fucking Vance," I said, pulling one of her cigarettes out of the pack and lighting it. Griz darted from room to room, her tail in the air, hair standing up all over her back.

"You don't want to know," I added, and before she could say she really did want to know—which of course was what I hoped she would say—she reached into the basket where she kept her mail and handed me a long white envelope. The red stamp of the postmark had faded into a series of pale pink blotches.

"What's this?" I asked.

She lit a cigarette of her own.

"You tell me," she said.

I slid my finger inside the envelope and sat down at the kitchen table. Setting the cigarette in the ashtray, I took a deep breath and held it, unfolding the thin white sheet of paper and holding it up to the light.

In a shaky hand, it read:

I said see, see what you have done . . .
You made me love you and now, now, now, my hair is gone.

A lock of hair slid down the paper and into my hand. Lena lifted it gently with her fingertips and turned her wrist in circles, the light glinting in the one thick tuft of blue-black hair.

For a fleeting moment, I forgot about the egg on my head, about the way Vance had buried his face against the bump in my scarf, about the way I'd felt as he pumped and snarled, the frantic way we'd clawed at each other. For a moment I thought only of Lena sitting in the living room with Ernie watching Elvis movies, of Ma reading books on Rogaine and longing for the days when it was safe to listen to "California Dreamin'," when the names of their children didn't smack to

Our Father of defeat. And Our Father sitting in a seedy motel, begging Ma to dance to an Elvis record in the dark.

"I don't think it's funny," Lena said, her eyes welling up. "I don't think it's funny at all."

Even though I knew she didn't believe me, I swore I hadn't sent it, that the only reason I made up the cards every year was to cheer her up.

"You've got to believe me," I said, touching her arm. "I'd never be so cruel."

She sniffled and wiped her eyes with the back of her sleeve.

"Yeah," she said. "Don't be cruel."

We both laughed then, and though I suspected Vance of playing a trick on us after the scene in the bedroom, I kept my thoughts to myself. I doubted he'd have had the sense to come up with a play on "See See Rider." Vance loved the early Elvis. The seventies tunes had escaped him.

"I have an idea who might have done it," I said, "but try not to worry. Besides, I have something more important to tell you."

I lifted the hair from her fingers and stuffed it back into the envelope. With pieces of Scotch tape I sealed the hair inside.

"I've got something on my head," I whispered, and before she could say anything, I pulled the scarf away and waited for her to say something.

She took a long time staring at me, finishing the last drags of her cigarette and stubbing it out in the ashtray. Then, just when I began to think she'd have nothing to say, she stood up from her chair, moved around the table, and cradled my head against her breasts.

We rocked slowly back and forth as she lulled me. Griz sat in the doorway as we hummed together, the bump quieting as we sang "See See Rider" softly to each other, our voices blending until I was no longer sure which one was mine.

I've often wondered which death was worse—Elvis in the bathroom or Mama Cass and the ham sandwich. At least Elvis was reading *The Scientific Search for Jesus* when he turned blue and collapsed; his mind was engaged. Maybe he even had a warning that this was it, the final moment. He might have hoped someone would find him with a house full of family and hangers-on. Maybe he even thought Christ would come leaping out of the book and give him CPR. But with Mama Cass, how awful those last few moments must have been as she choked all alone—a ball of ham lodged so tightly that no amount of air could seep into her throat no matter how hard she fought.

Once you have a horn, you have an inordinate amount of time to ponder such questions.

At times like these, even with the egg that was now growing to a point on my head—it took a while to realize it was a horn; information like that doesn't register easily—it was hard to believe Lena couldn't simply walk out the front door like anyone else and drive to the supermarket, pick up a trashy magazine and sit reading about celebrity liposuctions gone awry on her front porch. But then something would set her off—her internet shrink, a reference to Our Father, a casual remark about Boyd—and she'd be running from room to room begging for someone to help her before she died.

I asked her what those moments were like, and she said they were all similar when she was caught up in them. She understood it was her mind turning against her—an imbalance of serotonin, Vance said, a bit like what happens with baldness when the hair follicle receives no signals at all. She'd become lost in the feeling that her body no longer belonged to her, that life was a bad film filtered through a tunneling lens. She could hear, but the sounds were unfamiliar; you could touch her, but the contact of skin to skin didn't register the way she knew it should have.

"I know what being me feels like," she said once after Boyd left and the attacks came as often as ten times a day, "and I'm sure I'm going to stop being me right then and there. I'll never be me again."

I wasn't afraid—at least not at first. But the horn had allowed me to understand what not feeling like yourself really means. It wasn't one particular thing that made me who I was, not my role in restoring women's hair, not my having a sister who wouldn't leave the house or parents who had left. It wasn't just my looks, either. Something inside had shifted, making the me that I thought I knew all the more elusive. People make offhanded remarks to that effect all the time—"I just don't feel like myself today," or "You don't seem like yourself"—but if they knew how it truly felt to be sure you'd never be you again, they'd stop saying such stupid things; I'm convinced.

"You don't know what it's like to be afraid of your own head," Lena told me once.

How I wish we could relive that day. I'd take her in my arms and tell her, "I know what it's like. Now, I do."

TEN

Lena dyed Easter eggs to give to Ernie while we waited for Joan to arrive. She loved all the holiday rituals associated with Christianity but never tried to deter me from my own Jewish yearnings. I'd called Joan in the morning and asked her to pick up the loosest turban she could find at Regal's, one that would fall near the brow line and not cut into my skin.

"What did that toe-hacker do?" she demanded when I'd called to ask her for the turban, but I couldn't get into it with Joan, not then.

I left several messages on Ernie's answering machine while I waited for Joan to take me to my second appointment with Dr. Javits. I tried to be vague about the note, and I said that we'd be needing some extra help with the mail.

"Someone's left a terrible message for my sister, Ernie," I said just before hanging up. "I'm counting on you to make sure she doesn't get any more grief."

I promised Lena I would find out who had sent the note and that, for the time being, we should think about Elvis.

"Well, that's not a problem," she said, dipping her eggs in the colored water. "I do that all the time, especially at night when I'm scared."

Lena handed me a pink egg to match the one on my head, and smiled.

"You should try it, Cass," she said, setting the warm egg in my hands. "Sometimes it's really nice to think about Elvis."

I balanced the egg in my hand and smiled back.

"What exactly do you think about?" I asked.

She sighed, dipped one of the eggs in purple dye, and lit a cigarette.

"The usual things, I guess," she said. "I think about all the women screaming for him and the way he'd kiss the ones hanging on the edge of the stage. I think about why he liked staying in his house. I understand that. I think about what it must have been like to be Lisa Marie, riding around on the golf carts, how she must have felt like she never had her father all to herself."

I nodded and set the egg on the table. She blew out a full cloud of smoke and looked straight at me.

"But most of all, I think about what it would be like to be him. Even for just one day." She set her cigarette in the ashtray and swirled the egg in the dye with a spoon. "No wonder Rusty had a heart attack from trying. And Our Father, too. They just wanted a chance to get inside. Imagine what it would be like to *be* Elvis, you know?"

I almost said, "One never knows," but stopped myself.

She lifted the egg from the cup, the purple dye gleaming.

"I'll bet that's why they left," she said softly. "They wanted to know what it would be like."

I reached over and touched her hand.

"But he's dead, Lena," I said. "Elvis is dead."

She pulled her hand away and took a long drag from her cigarette.

"I know he is," she said. "Still, if that's what they left to find out, I just hope they did in some way."

I sat watching her while she decorated the rest of the eggs for Ernie, who had called to say he'd stop by later that night. I knew I could count on Ernie to be discreet about tracing the note.

While Lena finished her eggs, I wet my hair under the faucet and twisted a towel around it to drown out the extra noise that seemed to buzz all around me like static. Griz ran through the kitchen and batted her paws at Lena's legs every time Lena passed from the cupboard to the table where she'd set little teacups and dissolved colored tablets in vinegar and water.

"Maybe it's the cat," she said, as she dunked another egg into the green dye with the metal cradling stick that came with the package. "You're probably allergic. Maybe that's why your head swelled up."

I reached down to chuck Griz under the chin. She dragged her claws down my arm slowly, deliberately, as if trying to draw a straight line down my forearm.

Lena set a green and purple egg in the empty egg carton to dry and got me some peroxide from her medicine cabinet.

Griz leaped suddenly and ran for Lena's bedroom. I poured some peroxide down my arm and listened to it sizzle. When Lena turned her back, I dabbed some on the tip of the egg on my head, but felt nothing but a minor fizz—like a nice buzz from a glass of wine or a hit from a joint. I tapped my head with the egg Lena had dyed for me while she rolled the other eggs in strips of glue and then sprinkled them with glitter. The egg split in two against the bump on my head and left bits of cracked shell all over the kitchen table.

I once had a client who asked me if I could fashion a pompadour for her husband with pieces of synthetic hair left over at the end of the day.

I refused. I said I didn't know how, even though I could have done it.

I thought it would be wrong to conspire and help someone

else try to think they could be Elvis just by copying his famous hairstyle.

To prepare me for my follow-up visit, Dr. Javits told me that he would have to measure its growth—he stopped referring to the bump as a "blemish" or even a "growth" and had resorted to calling the egg "it."

"It will only get larger," he'd said on the phone, "if we don't deal with it now."

Then he wished me *shalom* and told me to come as soon as I possibly could.

Joan insisted on driving me, though I'd have preferred to go alone. She said I was in no condition to drive with a bump on my head that had no name.

"Maybe you fell and don't even remember it," she said, "or maybe that toe-hacker did something to you, and you've blocked it out. You could have amnesia, or a concussion, for crying out loud."

I wanted to tell her that something about this growth felt inevitable, as if I'd always known it might appear—just as Lena had known that one day our parents would leave us and that she'd seal herself up in the house—but Joan wasn't the kind of person to hear such things.

On the way to Javits's office, I insisted we stop at a supermarket for a box of *matzoh*. If Lena could pretend it was Easter, I said, then I could just as soon have my own little seder with Dr. Javits. I hated ham, and the truth was, I felt like a Jew. I wanted to be a Jew. Why should I continue to deprive myself of what I felt was my essence?

When I asked her to stop for some *challah* at a Jewish bakery, though, Joan said I was taking things too far.

"It's not going to last forever," she said, trying to calm me as I ranted on about becoming Jewish. "People have things like these removed all the time. Think about how many times you thought you couldn't do anything to save a scalp scarred from a bad transplant. Or how many times you've wondered if a client would be better off with a power perm than saddling herself with hair additions. Just ask that toe-hacker how many times he's removed toenails from people's feet. It's a walk in the park, if you'll pardon the expression." I did.

"I read an article that said Elvis was always searching for why he was born Elvis. You've got to stop torturing yourself," she said, as we pulled up to the office door.

"Joan," I said softly as I opened the car door, "this has nothing to do with Elvis."

"That's what you think," she said, and switched on the radio. The opening bars of "Jailhouse Rock" blasted through the speakers.

"Sorry," she said, snapping it off as quickly as she could. But it was too late—the song stayed trapped in my head all the way across the parking lot and through the front door, in the elevator up to the fifteenth floor.

Dr. Javits glanced at the *matzoh* before leading me into his examination room. I held the box to my breast, immediately embarrassed to have brought it. He measured the egg with his thumbs, sighing heavily.

"It's just as I feared," he said. "It's out of my hands."

I would have to see a surgeon now, Javits said, as he filled out a referral form. My egg was believed to be an "atypical cyst," something Javits could no longer treat in his domain of expertise.

"His name is Anderson, and he's quite well-respected," Javits said. "I couldn't leave you in better hands."

I stared at the name of the referral and felt my breath become trapped in my throat.

"Anderson?" I gasped. "What kind of *goy* name is that? I want a Jewish doctor!"

Dr. Javits smiled and patted me gently on the back. I had a sudden craving for Manischewitz. He got up to wash his hands while I fought to regain my composure.

"It's easy to dismiss Gentiles," he said. "They used to think we Jews had horns. Some people think this dates back to Michelangelo's *David*," he said, reclining in his office chair, "because of the horns on the statue. It was actually the result of a mistranslation of the word 'qeren' in Exodus, which actually means 'light.'" He smiled as I wound the turban around my head.

"Some people believe Michelangelo would have known better, though," he continued, "and that he put the horns on there as an act of defiance, to give Moses the air of virility and power. After all this time, who's to know?" he asked, and I said under my breath, "One never knows," but Javits seemed not to hear me.

There had been so many misinterpretations about Elvis. I thought of telling some of these to Dr. Javits, but kept quiet.

"Stay away from ham, and attend services regularly," he said as he showed me to the door. "This growth, it will be taken care of."

We shook hands and exchanged Good *Yom Tov*s at the door as he handed me the referral to a Dr. James Anderson, M.D. On the way out the door, I handed the receptionist all of my referral forms and said to myself the beginnings of the only prayer I knew.

Baruch atah Adonai, I thought, *Eloheinu melech ha'olam . . .*

I got into the car with Joan. We drove without speaking as I clung to the box of *matzoh* so tightly that the pieces cracked, the sounds echoing through the silent car.

The day before they left, Our Father spent two hours in the bathroom, having clogged himself up with too much of Ma's mashed potato-and-burnt-bacon sandwiches. I later learned that Elvis also suffered from severe constipation. It's one thing to know this about your own father, but it's another thing to know this about Elvis. Some biographers have even suggested that Elvis sat so long on the toilet because he was trying to relieve himself when he died, that he was "straining at stool." Since having lived through the horn's straining to be released, I've thought of the two of them struggling, Our Father and Elvis, their legs going numb from all the prolonged sitting.

I've often prayed that they found some relief in those moments.

Perhaps having a horn has increased my empathy for other people's suffering.

I went to Dr. Anderson's office alone. Joan had offered to take me, but I put her off on the ruse of going on a shopping spree for some new hats and turbans. She seemed wounded that I didn't need her, but when I explained the procedure, she agreed it was best. She couldn't bear to see anything hacked off, she said, even toenails. Although I winced a bit at the word "hacked," I thanked her for understanding that I needed to do this alone.

Excision, they called the procedure, like the extractions the aestheticians performed every day at Regal's, coaxing blackheads to wriggle free of oily skin under a mirrored light. I imagined the bump being held between a pair of pincers and squeezed until it burst from the skin, leaving behind a core of seeds— not unlike the plantar's wart Vance had once pulled from my foot.

"You must be Cass," Dr. Anderson said, eyeing my turban but making no comment. He led me to a small room with a light overhead and long needles spread across an immaculate countertop. He looked vaguely familiar and he stared at me as if he'd seen me before and was trying to place where and when.

"Have you ever been to Bagel King, down on Thirty-first Street, by any chance?" he asked, as I climbed on the table and lay back against the tissue paper.

"No," I lied. I couldn't picture a *goy* like him in a place like Bagel King. "I can't say that I have."

He readied his instruments and shined a light in the middle of my forehead.

"Well," he said, "you're a dead ringer for this woman who goes in there all the time. She never tells the guys her name, but is she a looker."

I closed my eyes and tried to swallow the smoky taste of lox in the back of my throat. I remembered him from the crowd of people, the way he'd looked me up and down in my minidress, the plain *goy*ish bagel with low-fat cream cheese he always ordered.

"Will this hurt?" I asked, trying to change the subject as quickly as possible. I slid the turban from my head and watched for his reaction, but his face remained unchanged. He covered my face with blue cloths, leaving only the bump exposed as he injected my head with a cold anesthetic.

He shook his head as the needle descended, the numbness ricocheting through my nose and across my cheekbones, up my brow line and down into my earlobes.

He lowered the needle and fastened a bandage to the bump on my head.

"I'm going to have to remove this," he said, helping me to a sitting position and discarding the blue cloths in a basket marked "Hazardous Waste." "Most times these things can be performed on an outpatient basis, but I'm going to have to sedate you. A Valium drip won't do, I'm afraid. This requires in-patient treatment. It's a very stubborn growth. It will take some time for me to remove it."

I pressed a hand to the egg and felt a cold shock through my hand.

"How much time?" I asked.

"It's hard to say," he continued, turning his back to me, the blond hairs curling at the back of his neck. "You'll have to miss time at work, and will be out of commission for a week, most likely."

He turned to me then and stared at my head.

"What is it that you do for a living?" he asked.

I covered the egg with both hands and reached for the turban. Bits of saliva clung to the sides of his lips. I wished he would wipe his mouth, and I even fished in the pocket of my jeans for tissues, but found only a ball of bluish lint.

"I'm a hair replacement specialist," I said. "I'm certified to help women regain their hair and feel better about themselves."

He lay a finger on his chin and nodded.

"So you and I are not so different after all."

He eyed the *chai* around my neck, leaning forward to get a closer look.

"It means life," I explained, my words coming faster than I intended them. "Lots of people wear them, not just Jews. Elvis had one, you know. He wore one all the time. Watch one of his concerts. You can see for yourself."

He helped me down from the table where I sat on a chair beside a low desk.

"You're an Elvis fan, are you?" he asked.

Suddenly my legs began to tremble beneath the table, and I had a vision of Elvis on Ed Sullivan singing, "Don't Be Cruel." I could barely hear my own thoughts, let alone grasp what he was saying about a specialized hospital for cosmetic surgery. The table wobbled as my legs seemed to dance of their own accord, and his voice became a warbled blur.

Elvis drowned out everything.

PART III

*Elvis was never prepared
to be what he was.*

—LAMAR FIKE,
member of the Memphis Mafia

ELEVEN

On the way home I began to piece together what Anderson had told me. I would be admitted to a hospital specializing in cosmetic surgery and skin disorders, the likes of which were usually seen in textbooks, he warned. He also thought it would be best if I told no one about the growth. If word leaked to others in the medical profession, it would surely stir up a frenzy among plastic surgeons. And then before I'd know what was happening, they'd convince me to have eye lifts, tummy tucks, even silicone breast implants, which, as far as he was concerned, he said, glancing down at my tight red blouse, I had no need for.

"When people ask why you're being hospitalized, don't reveal too much," he said. "Tell them you have a benign growth, which is actually the truth. And remember, security at this facility is tight. These are not people who want to be seen by the public."

I imagined lepers dropping fingers on their way down the hall, women with scars far worse than Ellen's battery-acid teardrops.

I was vague with Joan when she stopped at my house, as Dr. Anderson had advised me, telling her only that the bump was some type of cyst I'd have to seek special treatment for.

"I have to go away to have it removed, but then I'll be as good as new," I assured Joan when she stared at the wall, even though the honeymooners had gone quiet. "I'll need some wigs if you can get your hands on them," I said, "but don't tell Maureen what they're for."

"We're not talking amputation here, are we?" Joan asked, going pale.

I assured her there would be no such drastic measures. How could they amputate my head?

"It's a cyst, just like you said," I told her, getting her a glass of water. "They'll take it off, and that will be that. No big mystery. Just a common cyst."

Joan lit a joint, though I refused when she passed it to me for fear it might react with the anesthetic when they put me under.

"What did I tell you?" she said, taking a deep hit. "That toe-hacker's been filling your head with too many horror stories."

I kept quiet and fingered the soft fabric of the turban around my head, wondering what was going on beneath it.

When Joan left, I packed a suitcase and tried to set my affairs in order. I brought as many things as possible from my apartment to Lena's house, including the cat's bowl and toys, cosmetic cases and hairbrushes, tubes of gel.

When I finally finished packing and had written a letter to Maureen explaining my absence, I lay back on one of the twin beds, Lena on the other, and made her turn off the lights. Normally Lena was afraid of the dark and insisted on sleeping with a night-light, but when I told her how important it was for her to keep the secret I was about to tell her, she switched off all the lights and held her breath.

"It's a cyst, possibly even a tumor," I blurted. I knew Lena would ask fewer questions if I resorted to drama. "It's not malignant or anything, but I have to go to a hospital. It has to come off."

For several minutes she said nothing. I could hear sniffling in the next bed, the wet sounds of her fight to hold back tears.

"I knew it," she whispered finally. "I knew something would take you away from me."

She reached across the space between us and fumbled for my hand. I gripped her hand tightly, our fingers intertwined, our arms stretched between the beds the way we'd lain one night in our childhood bedroom when our parents had screamed that we'd ruined their lives, when Ma said that having us as kids had caused her hair to fall out in handfuls. We'd broken an Elvis record when we'd slammed the lid to the turntable while pretending that our living room was a disco, and had been sent to bed.

We should have seen it then, I thought, holding Lena's hand. *We should have seen it coming.*

While we lay there holding hands, I thought about how different I'd always felt from them, how separate, even since childhood. As much as I'd resisted admitting it, I'd envied Lena when she stopped going outside. Part of me wondered how it would feel to be trapped in a house or to lose my full head of hair. To be afflicted somehow. To not be the beautiful one.

I thought of whispering these things to Lena, but the buzzing in my head stopped me, all of my senses focused on the growth. Griz appeared and stared up at me, blinking, as if she understood. She jumped between us and moved to scratch at our arms, but at the last second she seemed to think better of it, and jumped up on the pillow beside my head, purring all the time.

Long after our parents had gone, I thought of little Lisa Marie standing outside the bathroom door screaming, "My daddy's dead!" while Vernon wept and the bodyguards begged Elvis to breathe. I imagined Our Father collapsing in the bathroom behind a closed door, Lena and I sliding Elvis records under the door to revive him. At his funeral we'd wear long wigs and sway back and forth at the grave site like Mama Cass, asking him to dream a little dream of us.

In the fantasy, Lena wept openly, but I couldn't, no matter how hard I tried.

I didn't cry when they left, though I think I wanted to—at least now, I wish that I had.

When we didn't answer the door, Joan left a package for me next to a box of assorted Elvis items Ellen Graham had left for Lena.

We opened our packages at the kitchen table. When she got a first glimpse of the Elvis watch Ellen had left her, Lena started to hyperventilate, but then she sat down with her paper bag until her breathing returned to normal.

"That wasn't so bad, was it?" I asked her. I had the wet towel on my head again to muffle the sounds of static buzzing in my head. "That one passed pretty quickly."

She nodded and dug out the contents of the box: an Elvis postcard; a mug with the phrase, "Thank you. Thankyouverymuch," in yellow lettering; a picture of a young Elvis in his G.I. uniform; and a pin that read simply: "Elvis Lives."

As soon as she'd finished, she lit a cigarette and puffed at it thoughtfully, blotches of redness from her near-attack still riding up her throat.

"I'll add these to the collection," she said.

My box was filled with long wigs that featured heavy bangs. Joan had lifted them from Maureen's personal supply closet. She'd given me one in each color—russet, chestnut brown, and deepest black, in case I couldn't decide which to wear. I already had an assortment of turbans, hats with bangs clipped to the front, and a long spool of dark hair we used for extensions. Maureen used the wigs as practice runs. There was a lot of romance surrounding long hair, Joan always said, but sometimes seeing yourself with a cascading mane was too unsettling when you'd worn it close-cropped for so long. Stuffed inside the box of wigs was a note from Joan on embossed stationery from Regal's.

Dear Cass,

I am so terribly sorry about your head. Try to think of Lena. I think she'll understand. Remember that she's not only lost your parents, she's lost her toenail, too.

I know I've never told you this before, but you're the best hair replacement specialist I've ever known. Regal's won't be the same without you. Neither will I.

Love,

Joan

P.S. Watch out for that toe-hacker. He's not who he seems to be.

I left after Lena had gone to sleep. Ernie had agreed to meet me outside after midnight in his mail truck so that I could give him the note we'd gotten with the lock of hair and instructions on how to take care of Lena while I was gone. She'd taken an extra Xanax to help her sleep after she'd talked to her internet shrink for over an hour. He told her to copy the words to Elvis's "Peace in the Valley" when her negative thoughts threatened to overtake her.

As she played the record over and over again, I wondered—if the lion and the lamb would lie down and the bear and the wolves would be gentle, what would happen to the rhino? Or to a woman with a horn on her head, for that matter?

The shrink had sent her two hyperlinks, one for Elvis fan support groups and one for siblings of people with benign cranial growths. Before he signed off, finally, at my insistence—I couldn't see what benefit she was getting from these sessions since she seemed to need more Xanax every time she logged off the computer—the internet shrink sent an instant message in bold letters.

Are you lonesome tonight, dear Lena?

Lena was right, I thought, as I leaned over her and pressed my fingers first to my lips and then to her forehead—I couldn't risk letting the growth on my head touch her—the world was full of Elvis freaks.

Before I left that night, I told Lena one last story about our parents. It's still one of her favorites:

The first time they heard "California Dreamin,'" our parents were at a diner down the street from where Ma lived, fondling each other under the table in a corner booth.

We never did find out why Ma loved that song even after my birth, or why the line about the brown leaves spoke to her.

I've always found the song depressing as hell, with all the talk about the sky being gray and the church—why didn't they stop into a synagogue, at least?—but Lena has always held on to the image of our parents' passionate groping while scarfing down soggy eggs.

I find it repulsive. What a spectacle they must have made. In any case, I tell Lena about Ma's putting her hand on Our Father's knee after "Hound Dog" ends.

That's the kind of diner I imagine it to be, a place where you can hear Ray Charles or Mitch Miller or even Lena Horne.

"What the hell kind of jukebox doesn't have 'Jailhouse Rock?'" Our Father says, and just then, "California Dreamin'" comes on. Ma squeezes Our Father's knee so tightly that he can hardly breathe.

They say nothing through the first verse, dropping their forks on the table and gripping fingers, then palms, swaying in a strange rhythm, not like the rhythm of the song, but something different, more primal. For the first time since they started dating, they forget about Elvis, and though they miss him, they realize that something irrevocable has happened.

Ma suddenly feels the urge to get up and dance right there in the middle of the diner among the people eating chocolate cream pie, but she can't with Our Father's hand pinning her to the booth. She untwirls the bun at the back of her head— this was of course long before the baldness—and sways back and forth, back and forth—and the kicker is, it isn't even a winter's day.

When the song finally ends, Ma pushes her hair behind her ears with her fingers and blurts out, "When we have a daughter, Fred, I want to name her 'Cass.'"

He smiles, and it's quiet for a long time. Then he takes a dime from his pocket and whispers to Ma, "Here. Go on. Play us some more Elvis."

Years later, when she's in labor with me and switches on the radio to hear a Mamas and the Papas song, she remembers that night, how they fell in love with each other and with Elvis. More than her labor pains, she tells people, it's that memory that makes her cry.

If I've done nothing more as a sister, at least I know that I told Lena a story that made Ma and Our Father appear right before her eyes. She could picture them right there, she said, sitting in the booth and kissing, waiting for their favorite Elvis song. As I kissed her good-bye that night, I wondered if I'd ever be able to comfort her that way again.

Ernie was smoking a cigarette in his mail truck while I loaded the car with the box of wigs, my suitcases, and makeup kits.

"When did you take up smoking?" I asked him as he opened the door to the truck and stepped out.

He stubbed the butt on the sidewalk and looked down at his feet.

"I only take a few puffs here and there," he said. "I spend half my day outside while she's in there smoking all alone," he said, nodding toward the house, "and it might make her want to come outside and smoke with me." He shrugged and looked down at the butt on the ground. "I smoke when I stop by sometimes," he said, "and she says it makes her feel less lonely when I smoke with her."

I wanted to hug him right then and there and thank him for everything he'd done for us—all the nights he'd spent watching Elvis movies with us, all the cards he'd sent secretly through the post office just to give my sister hope. But the bump on my head began to vibrate, and I had no words to say such things.

"Here's the letter I told you about," I said. "It must have come on your day off."

He brought the letter over to his mail truck and shined a flashlight on the faded postmark.

"I haven't been off in over a week," he said. "I don't see how this could have gotten past me."

He scratched at the mark in his hair where the mail cap left a permanent ridge and sighed.

"You know I wouldn't let this get near her," he said. "I'll put a trace on it right away."

We moved toward my car. He held the door open for me as I slid into the driver's seat.

"I wish I could tell you where I was going," I said. I adjusted the rearview mirror as Ernie clutched at the letter in his hand. "You know," I said, forcing a laugh, "doctor's orders."

He nodded and closed the door for me. As I started the engine, he handed me a piece of paper with his beeper number written on it.

"Here," he said. "In case you run into trouble."

I thanked him and started the engine, passed him my house key and backed out the driveway. As I pulled away, he stood waving at the curb, and I thought of Lena asleep among the laminated newspaper clippings and floss our parents had left behind, the Twister game under the bed, the letter in Ernie's hands. How strange it was, I thought, that of all the people in my life—Selena and her Yiddish, Ellen and her father dying over Sinatra, Joan, and even Vance—that the mailman—the deliverer of bad news—would be the one I would trust to watch over my poor sister, who lay sleeping while I slipped away in the night, just like our parents had so many years before.

TWELVE

There's no way to prepare yourself for the shock of entering a hospital where having a horn is the least of your problems.

I'm sure by now you have your own ideas about what sorts of problems I might have had, my parents being among the few.

My head's been opened up before.

See if you find anything, and then, if you feel like it, let me know.

Or don't.

It's all the same to me.

On my way to the hospital, I wore a long black wig with a multicolored headband to secure it firmly to my head. The hair hung down my back and tickled my waist whenever I turned my head. Since I couldn't listen to the radio for fear of another Elvis onslaught, I stopped periodically at the side of the road to check my reflection in the mirror. Twice I reapplied eyeshadow and powdered my cheeks with heavy pink blush. The tip of the growth pushed the bangs away from my face, creating a softly mussed look. I sang "Monday, Monday" with the windows down.

I was giddy. I felt myself swaying. I tasted ham in the back of my throat, sweet and honey-smoked.

When I pulled into the gate, I noticed that under the name of the hospital, "Castlewood," it also read: "A Rehabilitation Facility." I wondered if they treated addictions as well as the physical problems some of the people had. I walked up to the front door and handed over my papers to a guard, who looked me up and down with a leering grin. Despite the growth and the wig, some things hadn't changed.

Dr. Anderson was waiting for me at admissions with a clipboard and a *chai* around his neck. He nodded approvingly at my headband and wig and said it would be a fine disguise.

"You were right about Elvis," he said. "I looked it up. In fact, not only did he study Judaism, but all sorts of religions. He was always searching for answers, apparently."

I pressed the bangs against my head and felt the bump pulsate.

"Aren't we all?" I asked.

As we walked down the hall toward the ward where I'd be treated, he warned me not to be alarmed by some of the extreme cases I might see. Most patients hid their conditions in a variety of ways. I was to stay away from the clients with the most severe problems, though how I would manage that was unclear since I wouldn't be able to identify them. The staff and its doctors avoided the word "hospital," he said, because of its bad connotations.

"We prefer to think of them as clients or even customers," he said, smiling, "not unlike your spa."

I wanted to tell him that if they truly wanted to evoke the feel of a spa, they'd need to burn some aromatic candles or incense, but I stopped myself.

"I'm sure you'll assimilate quickly," he said, guiding me through a set of double doors marked "No Entry: Physicians Only." "Act as if you're one of the regular clientele, even though you're not." Then, turning his head, he muttered, "At least not yet."

"What?" I asked.

When he didn't answer, I blurted out a question.

"Do you do hair transplants here?" I asked.

I didn't know what made me say it, but as soon as the words came out of my mouth, my forehead began to sweat.

"You have no idea what we're capable of," he said, leading me to my room and laying extra blankets on the edge of my bed. "Transplants are barbaric. Here the hair follicle can be restored to its original potential." He smiled and pulled at the ends of his curls. "We've seen bald men—and women, too—grow a fuller head of hair than a king's. Look at me."

I did, and suddenly, as it registered that his blond curls were not real, that everything about him was false and springy, I felt an overpowering urge to jam my forehead against his shoulder and push him off the bed.

To stop myself, I turned away and fingered a loose thread on the blanket. As if sensing my sudden feelings of aggression, he stood up.

He would start with a chemical peel to loosen some of the growth, he said, before attempting to remove it completely. Cysts like mine could be stubborn, he warned, and I must have patience that all would go as smoothly as he promised. I thanked him and closed the door behind him, grateful to be alone. I lay on my quilted bed with my wig on and the headband squeezing the cyst. Sounds buzzed through my head, a series of low whispers I couldn't quite make out. As I tried to sleep, I reached into the pocket of my jeans and fingered Ernie's beeper number. Slowly I pulled out the slip of paper and clutched it in my fist, until my whole hand ached, my fingers sore from gripping it so tightly.

Rumors persist that Elvis had a nose job. Before undergoing the surgery—a rhinoplasty, and yes, even now, the word makes me shudder—he insisted that a longtime member of the Memphis Mafia have one first. I wished I could find someone willing to step in for me, get their horn removed, do a trial run.

But, of course, there was no one to ask.

I slept a dreamless sleep, the wig seeming to grow tighter during the night, and woke up early to take a shower. I was tempted to try a new exfoliating cream on the cyst but felt too unsafe without the wig. It created a shield from all the noises rattling around in my head. I couldn't bear to remove it, even for a few minutes. I washed it with a shampoo-and-conditioner combination I found in the bathroom, the kind set out on countertops in cheap hotels. On the bathroom door hung a white terry cloth robe with the Castlewood logo on it, a small castle with turrets and a surrounding moat. I put on the robe and then dressed in a pair of jeans and a loose blouse. When I was finished, I blow-dried the wig on my head, trying hard not to singe the edges with the heat.

When you've been kept awake by honeymooners' moans, a podiatrist humming Elvis songs, and the howls of your horny cat for so long, it's a great relief to be free of them, if only for one night.

With quilted cotton pads, I removed my mascara, washed my face with an aloe cleanser, and then applied a citrus-scented emollient. My skin was blotched around my eyes—the wig had cut off my circulation, I was sure of it, bursting a few capillaries along the way. I began with concealer before sponging on foundation, and adding a beige pressed powder. I looked—and even felt—oddly refreshed. With three shades of autumn shadow and blended eyeliner, even with a growth as large as an egg and a wig that clashed somewhat with my eyebrows' natural shade, I could still look good.

The nurse arrived to take me down to the solarium for orientation. She was a petite blond with breakage at her scalp, the result of too-tight ponytails, I guessed. I'd seen so much unnecessarily damaged hair at Regal's, but still it pained me each time.

"You must be Cass," she said, as we walked down the hallway leading to her office, a small room with a desk piled high with forms. Her frizzled perm begged for a hydrating shampoo. "I'm Sandra, and I'm going to be one of your nurses." She smiled and appraised the bangs on my wig. "Dr. Anderson has told me a lot about you. We've been looking forward to your arrival."

She had me sit on the table while she monitored my blood pressure, squeezing the rubber ball, the black velcro band choking my upper arm.

"I understand you're a hairdresser," Sandra said, scribbling numbers on my chart. I couldn't make them out no matter how much I squinted.

I tried to smile as she felt at my temples and around the glands under my chin.

"Hair replacement specialist," I said, eyeing the split ends that speckled her hair with whiteness.

She motioned for me to follow her to the door.

"There are certainly people who could use your services here," she said quietly before opening the door to another long hallway bathed in soft yellow light. "Although there are a lot worse things than hair loss, as you know, I'm sure."

She raised her eyebrows and smirked. Her hair smelled of cheap neutralizer, the waves crimped from using the wrong sized rods.

"Am I right?" she asked, staring directly at the point on my forehead where she clearly knew the horn lurked.

I thought about Vance and his bunion patients, how he'd sworn there was no foot he couldn't save.

"One never knows," I said, and followed her down into what she called "The Common Room."

They had their backs turned when I came in. Sandra warned me that some of the clients were friendlier than others, and that I shouldn't take it personally if I was ignored at first. Every afternoon, the clients gathered in the rec room to smoke and pass the time, waiting for their surgical procedures. Some clients had refused to speak to those not admitted to their inner circles, Sandra said, and it would soon become clear to me who went with whom.

"You'll find your own group," she assured me. "The new ones always do."

She warned me against removing my wig unless Dr. Anderson expressly advised me to. Most of the people made up their reasons for being there, insisting they'd suffered through bad electrolysis or face lifts gone awry.

"But don't be fooled," she said. "It goes much deeper than that."

She gave me a yellow pill—an antibiotic used as a precautionary measure before any procedure, she assured me—then led me to a table near the far end of the room where a group of women stood and smoked. Before I could tell her that I was only an occasional smoker, that I usually smoked only medicinal pot, Sandra slid a pack of Camels into my hand.

"You allow smoking here?" I asked, looking over at the cloud that hung over the women's heads. "In a hospital?"

Sandra looked around the room before leaning in toward me. "We don't use that word here," she said. "We prefer to call it a 'facility.'"

Then she tapped at the pack of cigarettes in my hand and whispered, "You're going to need these. They're a great way to make new friends."

I sat in a wooden chair at one of the unoccupied tables and stared at the cigarettes. *What kind of hospital encouraged smoking?* I wondered. I thought of the word "rehabilitation" on the sign outside, of Lena and her love of cigarettes that only sped up her heart rate, provoking more attacks despite her theory that the nicotine relaxed her. There was a bottle of mineral water waiting for me. How odd, I thought, to provide water and cigarettes, one so purifying, the other so damaging to the skin. I took a long sip and downed the yellow pill. For a long time I sat, fingering the cellophane wrap on the cigarettes until I finally opened them and began smoking.

On closer inspection, I saw that a group of five men and seven women stood by the windows that surrounded the room. They blew clouds of smoke at the glass. None of them glanced over at me or seemed to realize that I was there. When the silence became awkward, I cleared my throat several times, but still, no one turned.

I checked my watch, wondering when Anderson would send for me, though I'd forgotten to ask Sandra when my tests were scheduled. I wondered if the extra Xanax had warded off further attacks for Lena, if she'd fed Griz, if Ernie had kept watch from his mail truck parked by the curb. There were no phones that I could see. I felt suddenly woozy after I'd smoked a third cigarette, the room swimming with blue and yellow lines.

I was about to get up to pour myself some coffee from the urn I'd spotted on a table when a voice came from behind my head.

"They've gotten to her already," a woman said. "Those bastards."

I struggled to turn around to face her, but my movements were sluggish. Cigarette smoke swirled around me in snaking clouds. With both hands on the table to steady myself, I turned first my neck and then my shoulders, fighting to swing my body around. My head felt unbearably heavy, and I had the sudden urge to sniff coffee grounds up my nose.

Don't lose the wig, I thought, *don't lose your head,* and I felt the woman reaching for me with cold hands that smelled of rawhide.

"Where the hell is King when we need him?" someone yelled, and then my head fell forward, a loud crack sounding through the room as I fell forward and crashed into the table.

A sea of faces surrounded me when I came to. I blinked several times, trying to focus, and realized I was back in my bedroom. My hand moved toward the bump on my head, my fingers surprised to find the wig still secure.

"Is it over?" I asked the woman with thick pancake makeup who was leaning over me.

Nervous laughter rang through the room. The woman shushed them.

"Not by a long shot," someone said.

A pair of hands reached under my shoulder blades and helped me to a sitting position. I rubbed my eyes and coughed. The room moved in and out of focus. I felt my heart pound until I spotted my makeup case near the sink, the robe still hanging on the bathroom door.

"Am I out of surgery?" I asked, running my index finger over my face. I held my hand up to the light. Pressed powder stained the tip of my finger.

The woman with the pancake makeup motioned to some of the others.

"Let's get out of here," she said. "They're coming."

Together they hurried to the door and out into the hallway. Whispers tingled my forehead, spinning through the cyst.

"Where are you going?" I called, but no one answered.

I was about to get up to follow them when Sandra appeared in the doorway.

"You must have had an allergic reaction to the antibiotic," she said, pulling out my chart from the nightstand and writing notes on my chart. "That happens sometimes with new clients with delicate systems."

"But I'm not allergic to antibiotics," I said. I tried to sit up, but the effort caused the cyst to throb. "What was it that you gave me?" I asked, but she shushed me and pressed a cool compress over the bangs of the wig. Immediately the throbbing stopped, and I felt myself relax.

"We'll have to postpone the procedure, I'm afraid," she said, and then handed me a ballpoint pen. "Just sign right here that you've agreed."

I opened my eyes and looked at the mass of forms she held up in front of my face. All I could make out were the lines with xs next to them, one after another, page after page, where I signed my name and initialed until my head felt too heavy to lift it. For a brief moment I wondered what I'd signed, but the seams of the wig dug so tightly into my scalp that I fell asleep with Sandra's smiling face above me, her clipboard rattling as she left the room.

Some time later the woman with the pancake makeup shook me awake. She helped me to my feet without a word and even waited while I added a fresh coat of lipstick.

"Dinner," she said, as I trailed behind her, my head still pounding from the crash in the common room.

We walked down another long hallway that led to a dining room with an enormous mahogany table lined with large wooden chairs. The woman motioned to the seat beside her, and I took it, settling into the heavily cushioned chair. I recognized some of the faces I'd seen in the common room and smiled at them, but none of them smiled back. At the far end of the table sat a large wing-backed chair with what appeared to be rhinestones etched into the wood.

"Who sits there?" I whispered to the woman next to me.

She smiled for the first time and said, "It's reserved for King. We wait for him every night, but he very rarely joins us."

Just as I was about to ask who King was, a door I hadn't noticed suddenly creaked open at the far end of the room. My stomach rumbled.

The woman leaned in closer, her arm brushing lightly against mine.

"Feeding time," she said. "Take what you get, and don't say another word."

A long metal cart came rolling into the corner of the room, one pale hand grasping the handle. Something made me want to see the attendant, but others leaned forward around me, blocking my view. I tried to crane my neck, but all I could make out were broad shoulders under a white coat, a shock of black hair that flashed forward and then retreated through the closed door.

"Thank you," they said in unison. "Thankyouverymuch."

The others rushed toward the cart and took the food, which lay on heavy china plates embossed with the Castlewood logo. One of the women slid a plate toward me, and I stared down at the boiled potatoes and the slab of meat, the mountain of green peas. A hunk of bread fell on the carpet, and I leaned down to pick it up.

The walls were so white I could no longer see the door when it closed. The woman with the pancake makeup urged me to eat.

"Who was that?" I heard myself ask.

The others sat with their chairs pulled up tightly against the table. They ate hunched over without looking up. The woman inched her chair closer to mine and shoved a handful of peas into her mouth.

"That was him," she said.

The woman smiled to herself, her lips smacking as she bent over her plate. Grease lined the edges of her mouth.

I lifted the piece of meat on my plate with my fingertips. The growth pulsed as I noticed in horror that it was a thick slab of ham, dry and smeared with fat.

Elvis typically ate three cheeseburgers well done to the point of being blackened, and then several banana splits. When he talked too much or drifted off, the cheeseburgers would be systematically replaced. I've often wondered whether the banana splits melted, and if he ate them with the ice cream oozing out the sides of the dish, if the soggy bananas slid down his throat.

Elvis often ate in bed with a tray across his lap. He loved to eat in his pajamas.

I don't know how I know these things. Some of them Lena must have told me; some just come to me. I no longer think about why.

When I didn't touch my plate, the woman asked if she could have the piece of ham.

"I don't eat ham," I said. "Dr. Anderson should know that."

She raised her eyebrows as I handed her my plate.

"Oh, you're a Jew," she said, stabbing the piece of ham with her fork. "Anderson seems to like Jews."

She reached out to shake my hand, then pulled it away and wiped it on her white linen napkin. She was what Selena would have called a *zaftig* girl—large breasts and hips, curvaceous and meaty.

"He likes the pretty ones, too," she said. "But they never seem to last."

I wanted to tell her that I wasn't pretty anymore, but before I could say anything, she turned her attention back to her plate. After she polished off her portion and half of mine, she turned back to me.

"I'm Norma," she said. "After Norma Jean, you know, before she was Marilyn Monroe. It's not a name I particularly like, but I guess it's as good as any."

Norma had platinum hair with three-inch black roots. She wore a mole on her right cheek that looked as if it had been tacked on with a smudge of ash. The *shmutz* on her face spoke to me of her desperation. I thought of telling her how much more effective a black eye pencil or even a dot of mascara would have been, but she preened in her chair and smiled at me.

The others had lined up against the wall and had started pacing back and forth. A man with a limp led them to the left, then turned on his heel and followed as the woman on the other end of the line led them back toward the right. They moved in synch, as if they'd done this over and over again.

"I'm Cass," I said, but did not elaborate on the origin of my name.

Norma continued chewing pieces of ham. Her cheeks bulged, the ash floating down in specks from the space above her upper lip.

"So, what are you in for?" I ventured, reaching inside my breast pocket to check for the pack of Camels. They were still there. I could have fixed her mole and her bad dye job. I shuddered to think of the effects dirty ash would have on the skin's natural emollients or how much peroxide it would take to lighten her black roots. With hair that badly bleached, she might have been better off bald.

Norma dropped her fork and folded her arms over her large breasts. She passed a fingertip over the beauty mark, as if purposely smearing the mole.

"That's not something we discuss," she said.

I watched the line of people pacing back and forth. Each time they moved from left to right, I felt the growth tingling beneath the wig. As far as I could tell, the women had their own hair—no signs of wigs or integrations.

"When do we see the doctors?" I asked. "I'm supposed to have tests. Don't they run tests before they operate? Don't I consult with an anesthesiologist?"

Norma glanced over at the others. I could hear some of them humming from across the room. "Don't cry Daddy," one of the women sang to herself. "Daddy, please don't cry." I shuddered, ripples of sound moving through my forehead.

That was Lena's favorite Elvis song. My wig tightened.

"They don't do anything for a while, until all of the forms have been processed." She made an odd sound, a kind of grunting. "It takes time for all of the forms. There will be more for you to fill out, you'll see."

I slumped in my chair and stared at the group trudging to the end of the glass window and back again. How many times had they done this?

"You can pace if you want," Norma said. "I'm not one of the pacers."

I shook my head and lifted the pack of Camels from my pocket. Before I could answer her, the others were upon me, hands grabbing and tearing at the pack, breaking filters and shoving the cigarettes in their mouths. I managed to rescue the pack, popping a cigarette into my mouth and rearing at the crowd. They backed away suddenly and stared at the point on my forehead where the cyst raged.

"Don't come any closer," I warned, pointing my lighter at them like a weapon. "Stay back."

Several of the women glanced at Norma.

"It's o.k.," she said, raising her voice. "She's one of us."

I wanted to protest, to shout that I was a specialist in my field with a cat and a sister who needed me, that I had a podiatrist for a boyfriend—or maybe, by this time, an ex-boyfriend—that men of all kinds desired me, but it was clear no one was listening. We sat and puffed on our cigarettes, the clouds enveloping us and blocking my view of the glass beyond.

These are my people, a voice inside me said, though I couldn't figure out why.

You discover things about yourself once you develop a horn. You may find you like oatmeal after all, or that you judge people by the curve of their natural hairline. You may realize why your sister's husband left her, or why leaving the house could be so frightening.

You may miss Elvis. And, even if you hate them for the things they have or haven't done, you may even miss your parents.

THIRTEEN

The next day, after my morning shower and blow-dry with the wig still on, Sandra came to my room and told me that she needed more signatures. We took different turns down the various hallways than I remembered, and I began to feel a vague sense of panic that I would not be able to find my way back to the common room.

"Where are we going?" I asked. "I don't remember this way."

She just smiled and led me down another series of hallways.

"This is a very large facility," she said. "It can be confusing at first, I know. But we'll make sure you'll get to where you need to go."

I stopped near one of the stairwells on the right side and tried to open the door, but it was locked.

"Where's Anderson's office?" I asked. "I really think I should've been seen by Dr. Anderson by now."

Just then we reached her office. She held the door open and urged me to relax.

"Dr. Anderson cannot see you until all of your forms are in order," she said, as I sat down on a metal folding chair and looked at the clipboard filled with papers. "It's for your own protection that we take care of all of your forms."

The clipboard felt heavy in my hands. I let it drop onto my lap and glanced at the number of forms—fifty or more, I guessed—and took the pen she thrust into my hand.

"You just sign by all the xs," she said. "We try to make this as easy as possible."

Each paper had the name of Castlewood on the form as well as the logo of the moat in the upper right-hand corner. My name and address had been typed in on each sheet of paper in a large font, which got smaller as I read down the page.

"I don't get some of this," I said. "What does it say?"

She tapped at the desk with her nails and sighed.

"Oh, it's mostly repetitive," she said, "but unfortunately, each insurance company is different, and copies of the forms have to go to our many administrators."

I did see the words, "atypical cyst" and "excision," although most of the medical jargon escaped me. I signed my name on each of the dotted lines, so many that my wrist ached when I finally reached the end.

"There," Sandra said, standing up and taking the forms from me. "Now I'll take you back to the common room where you can wait. Once they're processed, we can get you started."

I followed her out the door and down another unfamiliar hallway, looking around at the series of closed doors that lined each new wall.

"What about telephones?" I asked. "I haven't seen one yet."

I noticed then that there had been no phone in the common room, none in the dining room, not even one in Sandra's office. Usually, I thought, based on my limited experience with hospitals, there were pay phones available.

"I'm afraid there are no outside lines at Castlewood," she said. "Dr. Anderson should have explained this to you. Security is very tight at this facility. He told me that you understood that."

We stopped at the entrance to the common room, and again I could not remember what turns we'd taken, as every hallway looked exactly the same—dim sconces on stark white walls, long rows of unmarked doors lining each side of the halls. None of the rooms, I'd noticed, posted either names or numbers. The cyst began to burn. I felt the sudden need to sit down.

"There, there," Sandra said, leading me into the common room and to one of the tables. She pulled out my chair for me. It was then that I noticed the opaque windows on both sides. As she went to get me a cup of coffee, I made sure to take note of the two exits on either side of the room.

"Try to relax, Cass," she said, setting the coffee and an ashtray in front of me. I started to push the ashtray away, but she pressed her hand into mine. "The best thing for a woman in your condition is to relax."

"With caffeine and cigarettes?" I asked. "I work at a spa. This is certainly not a way to relax."

Some of the other clients turned toward me and clucked their tongues. I looked away and sipped at my coffee.

"Our methods are unorthodox," she said, "but you'll see. They do work."

With that she turned on her heel to go, and I was left to sit alone at the table with nothing to do but smoke and wait.

It was hard to judge how much time had passed. After a while I could gauge it somewhat by the number of times the pacers moved back and forth against the wall. By my estimation, sixteen complete cycles—which I measured using the man with the limp farthest on the left, his feet seeming to be about a size twelve, which made the wall roughly fifty-eight feet long—equaled somewhere in the area of a quarter of an hour. I was good at guessing shoe sizes after spending so much time with Vance. He could measure a foot from fifty yards away. If you knew the measurement of your own foot, he always said, you could guess another person's size and even determine whether they wore a narrow or a wide shoe.

I'd never looked at people's feet so carefully. Vance, I thought, would have been proud.

Some of the men would nod in my direction every fourth turn, wetting their lips with their tongues like the men at Bagel King. It sickened me to look at them, so I focused on the women instead, though most of them stared right back at me, batting their eyes. Norma said it would take some time to be accepted, but before long, possibly before the next dinner hour, she would make some introductions. I wanted to tell her not to bother, that I'd spent half my life being leered at, but I decided not to alienate her.

She fluffed her hair at the roots. With the right shadow to give her the sloe-eyed look of a starlet, a thick coat of red lipstick, and what we call a "swell" perm to add some thickness to her hair, I could make her into a Marilyn double.

"The other clients can be fickle," she said, "but we look out for each other, and that's what counts. You'll need someone watching your back."

I reached inside the pocket of my jeans and felt for the slip of paper Ernie had given me. I thought of Lena and me in the twin beds, our fingers interlocked as we held hands across the space between. I promised myself that when Dr. Anderson finally came for me, I'd sign myself out of the hospital, call Ernie, and demand the name of a psychiatrist who could get my sister out of the house.

But Anderson never came.

When the pacers had completed nearly three hundred cycles, they headed back to their rooms to take their afternoon naps.

Two of the men stretched out alone in the corners, their size eleven shoes tucked under their legs, while others huddled together at various tables, staring at the opaque glass windows. One of the women got up and headed toward Norma and me. I sat with my back against the wall and stared at the glass.

The woman slid into a seat beside me and drew her knees up to her chest. Norma walked away and poured herself a cup of coffee.

"Sorry about your cigarettes," the woman said. Her hair had a natural virgin sheen, as if she'd never dyed or permed it a day in her life, the kind of woman the girls at Regal's loved to hate. "Most of the time we're pretty civilized, but with new people coming in, things can happen."

I nodded. She was the one who had been singing "Don't Cry Daddy." I shifted over an inch or two, subtle, trying not to scare her off.

"You must be Cass," she said, smiling. Her teeth were badly in need of a good flossing and some bleaching treatments from the dentist, but she had a kind of natural glow about her, the kind that comes with attention to quality shampoos and conditioners, cleansers without preservatives. "King told us you were coming."

I felt at the pack of cigarettes in my pocket. She leaned in closer and sniffed.

"How did he know?" I asked.

She laughed a little, her foul breath destroying the Ivory girl image she projected.

"King knows everything," she said. "There's nothing King doesn't know."

She stared at my wig and then down at the lump of cigarettes jutting out from my pocket.

"It's best to smoke when the others go off for naps," she whispered. "Most of them have a very strong sense of smell."

I offered her a cigarette and took the last one for myself. We lit them with cupped hands and blew thick clouds of smoke. She took off her shoes, a toe poking through a hole in her blue nylon sock. The nail bed was thick with calcium deposits, the edges of the toenail jagged and beginning to yellow. Fungus embedded in the nail could be serious, I thought, remembering the first signs of Lena's own bout. I wanted to recommend that she visit Rose for a thorough pedicure, but I realized I might not be seeing Rose again for quite some time.

She introduced herself as Janis. I thought of asking whether she'd been named after Janis Joplin or Janis Ian, but what did it really matter?

"Tell me, Janis," I said, careful to use her name the way I did at the spa. Maureen always stressed that using a client's name made her feel important, and by the light in Janis's eyes, I could see she was right. "When do the doctors come?"

She puffed thoughtfully on her cigarette and glanced around the room. Norma got up and moved toward the glass. Her blond curls had gone limp. I noticed that most of the pack wore long-sleeved shirts or turtlenecks. With my wig and short-sleeved blouse, I wondered how I fit in.

"They'll send for you once all the forms are completed," she said, leaning toward me, "and there are always more forms to fill out, in case you haven't noticed."

I told her about the visit to Sandra's office and the pile of forms, the promise that Anderson would treat me as soon as he could.

"They always send for the new ones, at least in the beginning, but then it's delay after delay. Something always goes wrong with the forms."

She inhaled deeply, holding the smoke for several long moments, the kind of inhaling that marks a practiced smoker. On closer inspection, the thin lines above her lip were more prominent. The sucking had clearly taken its toll.

"Now it's just King who comes," she said. "He brings the food and cigarettes and other things if he likes you. If you're a cooperative client and fill out all the forms without complaining, you can get more things when they send for you."

She clenched the empty pack of Camels and sighed.

"I'm sure they'll send for you," she said. "They always send for you at first."

I searched for signs of chemical burns or the rawness after dermabrasion on Janis's skin, but there were none.

I decided I had nothing to lose.

"What are you in here for?" I whispered. The wig itched, stray hairs prickling the sides of my face and irritating the back of my neck. I wanted to tear it off and dig at my scalp with my fingernails, but I remembered Dr. Anderson's warning.

She looked at me for a long time then scanned the room, looking over one shoulder and then the other, glancing nervously at the glass. Without a word she stretched her arm out in front of her and slid the sleeve of her turtleneck up ever-so-slowly. The bones of her wrist jutted out, pale and knobby, bits of dark hair sprinkling her upper arm. As she eased the sleeve above the elbow, she looked away from me and held out her arm.

Stripes. Her entire arm above the elbow was layered in black stripes.

Before I could say anything, the door at one end of the room clanged open. The people left in the room ran toward the glass and cowered.

"Janis, what have you done?" Norma screamed, spilling her coffee on the tile floor. "You know the rules!"

Men in white coats stormed toward us. They snatched us by the arms and dragged us toward the door. Janis thrashed and thrashed, digging her nails in one of the men's arms and clawing at him. I fought to free myself, twisting my body and shouting for them to let me go.

"Dr. Anderson!" I screamed. "I want to see Anderson!"

But they gripped my arms tighter and pulled me through the door into a dark room, bolting the door behind me.

Elvis's bathroom offered him a personal sanctuary, a place to seal himself off from the Memphis Mafia, the endless crush of fans at the gates, the din of all the comings and goings of the servants and the hangers-on. They say he had a barber's chair in his bathroom, and he often sat in the chair to sit and think or read one of his many books.

When I picture him in the barber's chair, I imagine heavy towels tacked up to cover the mirrors, as if he were sitting *shiva*. As vain as he might have been—and some say he once dyed his eyebrows so black that his eyes teared with infection—there must have been times when he wanted to forget how he looked, even before his face turned pasty and swollen. Sometimes, before his body filled with fluid and his looks turned against him, he must have been sick of looking like Elvis.

At least that's how I would have felt.

I sat in the dark for hours—or what seemed like hours. There were no clocks, no windows, no sunlight to measure the amount of time that passed. I thought about a game that Lena and I played as kids. We'd sit on the front lawn and watch the sun draw shadows on each other's faces and try to guess the time. At two o'clock the sun blazed in Lena's eyes; at three, she said, my nose formed a shadow above my lips. She didn't like to play the game very often, and would always want to quit at four o'clock.

"Let's see what happens at five," I'd plead, but she'd run for the porch and fling open the screen door, our game ruined by the scratchy sounds of "Can't Help Falling in Love."

Even then, I couldn't understand why she hated being outdoors too long. It wasn't as if Ma or Our Father paid much attention to either of us. And there were always the Elvis records to contend with.

Once, after Lena went into the house, I pretended to climb the stairs to my room but crouched down on the staircase instead. Our Father had gotten up from his recliner and had Lena by the hand, leading her in a slow dance. She was beaming up at him, and he was talking to her softly, with his lip curled, his belt buckle altered from his initials to read instead, E.P.

"You're my little Lisa," he said, "my little Lisa Marie."

Before they could find me spying, I crept up the stairs and rummaged through Ma's drawers for her makeup case. In the closet, hidden behind the box that held her wedding gown, I found the black wig I'd seen her wear one night very late when I was supposed to be sleeping. She'd been posing in the teased black wig, my father laughing in a throaty voice.

"Come on," Ma had breathed. "Come and love me tender."

I stood in front of the mirror and plopped the wig on my head. It was loose and hung down my brow if I moved my head forward, but with a few dozen bobby pins, I fastened it so tightly, it didn't budge at all when I twirled around. Then I painted my lips with a gluey red lipstick and pasted false eyelashes on with Elmer's glue. Slowly, deliberately, as "Hawaiian Wedding Song" played, I descended the stairs, one hand on the railing, and sauntered into the room, Ma's dressing gown dragging dust balls behind me.

Our Father dropped Lena's hands when he saw me, his lips curled back in a snarl.

"I want to play, too," I said, one of the eyelashes getting stuck to my bottom lid and making it hard to see. "Guess who I am? I'm Cilla."

A blob of glue from the false eyelash clouded my eye, and before I could rub it away, Our Father grabbed the record off the turntable and spun it across the room. I watched it sailing toward me. My heel caught in the seam of Ma's dressing gown as I tried to duck, and all at once we came tumbling down— me and the record and the wig flying off of my head. When Ma rushed in from the kitchen, she found me on the floor, face down. When she pulled me up, she shrieked that Our Father had made a grave mistake treating an Elvis record that way.

Later, when Ma made me sit for an hour with a pack of ice pressed to my head, I watched Our Father rocking back and forth on the front stoop, smoking and holding the broken pieces of the record in his hands.

That is one of my most vivid memories of childhood. Now you know why I'd rather not think about it.

By the time the door finally opened, I lay slumped against the wall. What a mistake I'd made by lying to Lena and even to

Joan, letting them think the growth was a benign cyst or some sort of tumor. If I'd told Ernie the name of Castlewood, at least he might have sent someone for me. Even after Vance's Elvis impersonation, I'd have been glad to see him. I'd have let him sing "Blue Moon" to me in a hideous falsetto. He might not have been the most sensitive man, but at least he'd have cared enough to look for me.

A sheen of bright light filtered through the room. I held my hands over my eyes as a woman approached, her heels scuffing the floor.

"The doctor wants to see you," she said, reaching down to cup my elbow. "You have to come with me."

She helped me to my feet and toward the door. Every time I opened my eyes, the light burned, so I kept them closed, holding onto her elbow like a blind person. The growth had finally stopped throbbing, and my head felt oddly detached from my body, as if it were no longer mine.

She fumbled in her pocket with a set of keys and opened the door to a room with a long table covered in sheets of paper. I rubbed my eyes as she sat me in a chair and patted my shoulder. Her back was turned. Beside the sheet of papers lay a pencil, my name stamped on the top of every sheet.

She turned to me then and smiled. I gasped, my hands flying up to my wig.

"I know you," I stammered. "I just did your extensions."

She smiled at me and touched the back of her long braid.

"Yes," she said, "I'm your Cousin It."

I held my face in my hands.

"It's all right," she said, smiling. "I know what you girls call me."

I struggled to lift my head and meet her eyes.

"Crystal," I said, "your name is Crystal, and you work with people who are *meshuge*." I cleared my throat. "I mean, the mentally ill."

She pressed a finger to her lips and squeezed my hand.

My God, I thought in a rise of panic, *after all the years of caring for my agoraphobic sister, I'm the one in the nuthouse.* No wonder all anyone did was smoke, I thought. In all the television shows or films I'd ever seen about mental hospitals, the patients always chain-smoked.

"I never said that," she whispered. "I only said the people I worked with were not what you'd call normal."

She handed me a cool washcloth to wipe my sweating face.

"My hair has never felt better," she whispered, glancing over her shoulder at the mirrored glass behind her. "Remember the first time I came in there with pieces missing all over my scalp? You saved me from all that. I'm a whole new woman."

She lifted one of the longest extensions and then let it fall.

"No one can ever tell that all this hair isn't really mine," she said. "There's something to be said for giving people a false impression, don't you think?"

Her smile broadened, revealing a set of crooked teeth.

"Can you get me out of here?" I whispered.

The rawness of my hairline burned as I tried to shift the wig into a more comfortable position.

"Just do what they say," she told me. "Let them look at you. Don't ask too many questions. For a while, all they'll do is look."

"It's a fucking zoo in here," I said, feeling the growth beginning to quiver.

"Oh, Cass," she whispered. "You have no idea."

She turned on her heel and headed out the door, locking me in behind her. I jumped up, knocking my head against a wall and then falling on my back.

"Wait! Wait!" I called. "I can do your extensions for free! I can make sure you never have to worry about your hair again!"

But no matter how hard I banged, no one came to the door. In utter defeat, I pulled the wig off my head and lay with it curled against my stomach, the nylon hair scratching my arms.

It was a fucking zoo, and Cousin It seemed to be my only hope.

FOURTEEN

An Elvis Questionnaire

1. *Why do you believe Elvis lived and his twin, Jesse Garon, died?*

2. *Why did Elvis continue to wear jumpsuits even after they were no longer an attractive fit?*

3. *Why did Elvis shoot any television set showing Robert Goulet?*

4. *If you could be one incarnation of Elvis, which would you choose?*

    (a) pre-famous Elvis as a teenager at Humes High School

    (b) the Elvis of the Ed Sullivan *special when he was proclaimed "a decent, fine boy"*

    (c) leather-clad Elvis of the 1968 comeback special

    (d) jumpsuited, tanned, thickly-sideburned Elvis of Aloha in Hawaii

    (e) drugged, karate-kicking Elvis of 1976- 1977

    (You may choose only one Elvis. State your reasons why.)

5. *If Elvis had survived that fateful moment in the bathroom, where do you think he would be now?*

Bonus Question: *What are your thoughts on the Colonel? Was he responsible for Elvis's worst career decisions, or did he truly want the best for his "boy"?*

In the space below the questionnaire, I wrote:

Don't look to me for answers. Everyone has their own ideas about Elvis.

Answer to Bonus Question: Fuck the Colonel.

I laughed as I wrote this last line. It had become one of Lena's and my favorite sayings, after that awful day when the news came on that Elvis was dead. Our Father had lain slumped in his chair, screaming at the television set.

"Fuck the Colonel! Fuck the Colonel!" was all he would say, until Ma brought him a glass of vodka with ice and a water pistol, which he promptly aimed at the television set, soaking the screen.

As I sat there alone in the room, I thought about my life since our parents had gone, since Lena had taken to drowning her sorrows in chat rooms and Xanax. I imagined Lena watching the Home Shopping Network and waiting for our parents to call in and order a collectible Elvis plate or brass hound dog. I thought about Vance and how little he really knew me. Every time I tried to describe how it felt to restore a woman's hair, he'd start in about calluses and bone spurs, how he'd suffered over the loss of people's toenails. I saw the salivating men at Bagel King, hoping to serve me lox and to finally learn my name. I wanted to smoke a joint with Joan, the only person I could really relax with.

Most of all, I saw the women beaming at their reflections in the mirror after I had used all my skills to transform the plainness of their everyday lives.

But I had been the one transformed.

I suddenly felt as if someone had gripped my head, squeezing it in a vice, the whole room spinning, darkness snaking through the bump and down through the length of my body. I struggled to stand, feeling my way along the walls, as the lump seemed to twist around and around itself, as if my head might spontaneously combust. I felt myself snort, my feet scraping the floor, long streams of mucus sputtering on the front of my blouse. Everything that I was, everything that I ever hoped to be, seemed to be trapped in the confines of my head.

Just when I thought I would black out, that the darkness would overtake me, I felt a surge of adrenaline course through my body.

They won't come for me, I thought, frantically. *No one is going to come for me.*

A pulse of light shot through my head, and I ran for the door, bending my head low and bracing myself for the impact. I rushed toward the door headfirst, banging it with my forehead with all of my might, mucus dripping in thick clumps. Once, twice, three times I banged the door, my whole body rearing back with the effort. Again and again I raced toward it, grinding my head into the cold metal, twisting my neck and charging the door again.

And then, as the door opened and Cousin It—Crystal— appeared with Dr. Anderson and a row of men in white coats behind her, I charged.

I ran straight for them, butting them with my head, knocking down first Cousin It and then Anderson, and then the other doctors. The group of them in their white uniforms toppled like bowling pins.

I lunged at the row of security guards who gripped their nightsticks and stared at me. Ignoring the chorus of voices behind me, I ran as fast as I could, the bump leading me as if a force were gripping it and pulling me along, as if I couldn't stop myself if I tried.

Just as I thought I'd made it to the front doors where I'd been admitted, where Anderson had stood with his *chai* around his neck and spoke to me about atypical cysts, I felt the dart pierce my lower leg. I fell at once. A crumpling wave of pain shot through my leg and up through my groin. For several steps I crawled, head down, hands pawing at the floor to drag myself forward. Everything around me whirled around in a crazy wave of gray and yellow dots.

I had been caught.

PART IV

Elvis was like a prisoner.

−RED WEST,

Elvis's former bodyguard
and coauthor of *Elvis, What Happened?*

FIFTEEN

It was three days before I was returned to the others. Anderson had placed me in a small room under blaring lights and told me I had a tumor that was quickly overtaking my face.

"We think it best that you don't see yourself for the time being," he said, standing several feet away from me and twirling the chain that held the *chai* around his neck. "For a woman as attractive as yourself, a tumor as rapidly disfiguring as this one could be especially devastating."

I'd nodded silently as he explained that I would be returned to mix with the others as long as I kept my head covered. He placed a long black veil over my face and led me down the hallway to Crystal, who seemed prettier than I'd remembered her as she carried packs of cigarettes in her pockets and refused to glance at me. Late at night, she'd crept into my room, slipping some of the forms, including my diagnosis sheet, and a compact mirror into my hands.

"You've always made me feel pretty, every time I've come to you," she'd said, as I caught the first glimpse of myself in the mirror. "This is the least I can do."

Patient Name: Cass Baine
Age: 35
Allergies: Pork-based products including (but not exclusive to) a violent reaction to deli-style ham.
Employment: Hair Replacement Specialist

Marital status: Single

Referred by: Harry R. Javits, M.D.

Medical history: Rash on buttock and thigh area believed to be caused by contact with bacillus in public toilet. Treated with fungal ointment and tetracycline. No recurrence. No history of acne, boils, or other eruptions. Uses retinol-based products for cosmetic purposes. No past dermal or epidermal disorders known.

Relevant family history: Little known of parents, though history of obsessive fixation on singer Elvis Presley resulted in parental abandonment. Loss of hair—possible case of alopecia (mother); agoraphobia/panic disorder, chronic fungal condition restricted to toe area (sister). Sister under the care of several psychiatrists and noted podiatrist, Vance Masterson, M.D. No history of melanoma or benign growths in immediate family members.

Current condition: Nonfungal epidermal protrusion at center of forehead; circumference 9.35 cm; diameter 4.2 cm; length: 16.77 cm. Discoloration of dermis at base; epidermal erosion at connection with forehead and at uppermost point of protrusion. Believed to be atypical cyst.

Patient indications: Patient notes increased libido in partner, minor disorientation and dizziness upon sudden movements. Indication of throbbing at tip of protrusion and through the surrounding dermal points.

Past treatment: Scraping performed; no fungal presence found. Antibacterial ointment and high doses of penicillin prescribed.

Observations following treatment: Continued growth of protrusion.

Results of biopsy: Evidence of keratin; hair follicles at dermis base.
Diagnosis: Horn.

I should have been surprised. A normal person would have been. But who can tell what's normal when there's a six-inch horn jutting from your forehead?

When they brought me back to the room with the two-way glass, the others backed away. Even the pacers stopped in midstride and shuffled off to corners. Some of the men recoiled and whimpered quietly to themselves. Norma, who had earlier been the friendliest of the group, got up from her chair and sat in the corner with her ankles crossed and her knees bent, not daring to look at me.

Crystal—I vowed never again to call her Cousin It—gave me ten packs of Camels and sat me in a soft, upholstered chair in the center of the room. Her long stringy extensions covered her face. The hair was badly in need of a tightening, and I felt a lump in my throat at seeing it so limp. She backed out of the room and disappeared behind the glass, leaving me no way out.

A horn is believed to have aphrodisiac properties. Cousin It had written this on the bottom of the form and had signed her name in swirly black ink.

As I sat among the others in the long black veil, puffing smoke through the nylon netting, I thought about how I must have looked staring at myself in the tiny mirror, turning it at different angles to try to collect the different spheres of my face into one complete picture. My eyes were turned down at the corners, bluish veins circling the sockets and on each side of my nose, sloping inward at the tear duct. The horn—*my* horn—curved and pointed toward the ceiling, forming a per-fect arc from the middle of my forehead up toward my hairline.

As I stared at the horn, I wondered how it would feel to have people look at me, not because I was pretty, but because I was different, different even from the others with stripes—and God knew what else—hidden under long sleeves and high-necked shirts.

With the veil draped over my head, I sat completely still while the group gathered around me in a circle. They sang to me in throaty voices an Elvis song I'd heard long ago about all the things a little girl might like to be. As the music floated through my head, I lifted the veil, and slowly they came forward, warily at first. Their voices grew stronger as they gazed at the horn. When the song was over, they stood at attention.

"Isn't it beautiful?" they whispered.

Then slowly, one by one, they bowed down.

I wonder if my parents had it in them to love an ugly child. It seemed, looking back, that they only paid attention to me once I'd hit fifteen and my looks had changed. Lena had never been beautiful, but she had silky hair and shining eyes. And, of course, she had those beautiful feet.

Once Ma's hair fell out, she'd become ugly. It wasn't just because of the lack of hair, but because of the unhappiness that had taken over her face. Even Our Father looked at her as if he'd lost all hope.

The fans loved Elvis even after his looks had faded. They'd never seen him for what he'd become—drugged, depressed, distorted. They still saw him the way he had been—full-lipped and lovely.

There's no happiness in a dead Elvis, no matter what they try to do to preserve him.

Later the group of pacers led me to the dining room. Two of the men held my arms at the wrists while the women shuffled slowly behind me. We took our places at the mahogany table. One of the men pointed at the rhinestone chair at the head of the table, but I shook my head slowly and did not move. When the metal cart appeared at the doorway, they all turned to me. Norma had been the one designated to usher in the cart and distribute the food because she'd been in the room the longest, and the others were keen on seniority.

"Norma is the only one who speaks to King," one of the women had confided the night before while sitting at my feet. "She has a way of getting things done that King responds to. They're both very old school."

I had no idea what this meant, but the woman—who introduced herself as Ann, as in Ann-Margret—seemed to know the others well enough to be an authority.

I felt intense pangs of hunger for the first time in days. Ann sat alone in a corner, her red hair marred by dark roots. The horn weighed my head down and made my neck slope forward, as if I were in a permanent state of prayer. My vision was blurred, yet sounds were amplified. I could hear the rhythm of every breath, every sniffle, every stifled yawn.

With my eyes turned up, I could see the tip of the horn poking at the veil. The others sat silently and stared at me, waiting for a sign.

"They want to know if I should still be the one to collect the cart," Norma said, her eyes downcast. "King can come no farther. We have to go to him."

The horn made my head unwieldy. My shoulders sloped forward to support it. With one hand pressed to the back of my neck, I managed a brief nod. The others cooed as Norma scurried toward the cart. She stood whispering at the doorway, nodded furiously, then grabbed the handle and dragged it rattling across the floor in front of me.

Among the slabs of ham on china plates sat one piece of sparkling china covered by a gold lid. Norma bent at the knee and slid the plate onto the table in front of me.

"This one is for you and you only," Norma said, her hands shaking as she handed me a linen napkin embossed with lightning bolts. "King was very specific about that."

I removed the lid slowly, the others holding their breath.

"What is it?" someone whispered. "What did she get?"

A toasted sandwich lay in the middle of the plate, the crusts of the bread slightly burnt at the edges.

I lifted the plate to my face and sniffed, but the horn had caused my mucus membranes to fill and swell, my breathing labored if I inhaled too deeply. It could be ham, I thought with a start, and nearly dropped the sandwich, but was suddenly so ravished that I closed my eyes and bit down.

Warm slivers of banana swirled in my mouth, the tang of peanut butter coating my tongue.

"Thank you," I said, my voice thick.

I said it louder, raising the sandwich in the air and waving to the others to take their plates.

"Thankyouverymuch," the others repeated.

A pale hand wiggled its fingers at the doorway and then disappeared, as the others chomped at their ham. The peanut butter stuck to the roof of my mouth and stayed there, long after the others filled and refilled my cup with water. When the sandwich was gone, I wiped at my lips carefully. Inside the napkin, folded in the corner, I found a tuft of hair, and beside it, the letters T.C.B. in a fine hand-stitching, small and delicate next to the hair, black and shiny as any I'd ever seen.

That night they stood guard in my room. They told me their names in strangled whispers—Spencer, Montgomery, Ella, Audrey—and sat at my feet, looking up starry-eyed at the veiled horn. Several times I urged them to return to their rooms to rest, but they refused, taking turns standing at the door while others sat with their backs against my bed. I tried to sleep but was awakened repeatedly with thoughts of Vance. My horn burned at the tip, my head filled with sweaty dreams.

I heard them long before they shined their flashlights on the tangle of bodies on the floor. The smell of sweat floated through the air in a sour cloud. When I heard the rustle of the doctors at the end of the hallway, I sat up and cleared my throat.

"They're coming," I said, my voice raspy but controlled.

Two of the men got up from their places on the floor and moved toward the hallway.

"When?" one of the women called. "When are they coming?"

Norma came and sat at my right side, Ann at my left.

"We won't let them take you," Norma said.

But I wasn't worried. I fingered the *chai* around my neck and raised my horn in the air.

"I don't hear anything," Ann said, sidling closer to me. "How do you know it's them?"

I pulled the veil tighter around my face and sighed.

"I see them," I said. "I see it all."

And I did, though the act of seeing was not what it had been before the horn. Images raced in a blur of color. I saw them moving down the winding hallways in a tight group, Anderson in the lead, the guards swinging their flashlights that scanned the dark rooms as they passed. I saw Lena asleep in her bed, dreaming of my funeral, waking up in a sweat just before the casket closed. I saw Elvis choking on a carpet, his tongue blue between capped teeth. There was no need to be afraid, I thought, reaching up to touch the horn, my fingers moving along the ridges. Everything had changed.

Slowly, as the doctors approached, the others herded around me. Even in the darkness, they wouldn't look directly at me. But I could feel their fists twisting in their laps, the urge to reach out and touch the horn sending shivers of excitement through their bodies.

When Anderson reached the door, the rest of the group stood. At first they were quiet, breathing heavily through their noses, the room suffused with the wet fog of their breath. Anderson pushed his way through the door with the guards at his side, the flashlight blinding some of the more timid ones. I smiled to myself and called out to Anderson.

"You've come for me," I said. "You stupid *goy.*"

I got to my feet, steadying myself against Norma and Ann. They gripped me by the elbows as I fought to keep my head erect. Anderson approached. The guards held back, their flashlights dangling in their hands.

"Yes, Cass, it's time to look into what's happened to your head," he said. "We've given you time to rest, to acclimate yourself to our facility. The forms are complete. And now something must be done. As a doctor, it is my duty to do this for you."

I motioned for the men to come closer. One of the older guards, a white-haired gentleman, had masturbated in the men's room earlier that day. I could smell it on him, the thick stench of his release. He would not touch me, no matter how desperately he wanted to. I knew this just by looking at him.

Norma helped me stand on a chair in the middle of the room. High above the crowd of bodies, I saw a brief spark of fear light in Anderson's eyes. He shifted his weight from one foot to the other, like a child about to wet his pants. He motioned to the guards to move forward. Just as they began to take their first steps toward me, I removed the veil, the black netting floating softly to the floor.

The guards gripped their chests as their flashlights rolled toward us.

"Put it back on!" Anderson yelled. "Put the veil back on!"

Norma lifted one of the flashlights and aimed it toward my face. I turned to display my profile, my horn leaving a magnificent curving shadow on the wall, the tip reaching all the way to the ceiling.

"No," I said, pointing the horn toward him in defiance. "Don't come any closer."

The guards lay on the floor, covering their faces with their hands.

The others stared up at me, their necks craned. Anderson took several steps forward then backed away as the crowd lunged. Some of the men growled, women spat, and Norma and Ann bared their teeth.

As Anderson retreated, he cursed at the guards.

"What are you staring at?" he yelled at the group. "Go back to your places! You know the rules!"

Slowly, the guards began to crawl on their bellies toward the door, Anderson kicking them in the ribs as they slithered away.

"What the hell *was* that?" one of the guards asked, stopping briefly in the doorway. "That sure as hell was not in my job description."

As the guards fled, the bolt sliding heavily in the door, I could hear someone crooning from far away. At first I couldn't make out the words, but then the others swayed back and forth in front of me. "Are you lonesome tonight?" they sang. They knelt before me, heads bowed. I settled into my chair and allowed each clammy hand, each trembling finger to stretch out toward my head and touch the horn. It vibrated at each point of contact. Soon they were amassed on the floor, rubbing themselves and each other, all of them singing Elvis songs in strangled voices. I sat with my face covered by the veil, while they told me over and over again how beautiful I was. I lit one of the cigarettes they passed to me, blew perfect smoke rings at the ceiling, and wept.

SIXTEEN

Why I was chosen to be given a horn, if "chosen" is the right word (I think it is)?

It's an understandable question, one I've asked myself many times. Sometimes, in order to truly understand, you have to get beyond the obvious.

Pry, if you want to.

But then, move on.

We moved back to the dining room for safety. Once inside, the men removed their shirts, and many of the women stripped down to bras and panties. At first I looked at them through the veil, not quite trusting what I saw, but then I asked them to line up against the wall, tossing my veil around my shoulders and inspecting each one.

Some had snakeskin that covered the fine hairs of their chest. Others grew long hair from their forearms, thick and wiry as an ape's. Pointy teats hung from one woman's midsection, milk droplets running down her legs. The wooly thickness of a sheep wrapped itself around another woman's neck.

I ran my fingers over the fine hairs of a horse's mane; the spots of a leopard, like tattoos, on one man's heavy belly; and the hooves of a young woman with—you'll forgive me—coltish legs. As I fingered the orange feathers that lined the wrists of one woman, she looked up at me, her mouth quivering.

"Why?" she asked. "Why has this happened to us?"

I laid my horn briefly against the top of her head. At least she could hide under turtlenecks and gloves, I wanted to tell her. There were others worse off than us.

Only Norma remained fully clothed. She sat cross-legged by my chair and waited for me, her head lowered. Her roots had grown terribly black. A tuft of red feathers sprouted from the part in her scalp.

"My mother wanted me to be Marilyn Monroe," she said, taking thick gulps of air to choke down her sobs. "But all I've ever been is a bad Norma Jean."

She lifted her face, the ash mark where her mole had been just a smudge on her left cheek. The red sprout at the top of her head looked like the beginnings of a hen's crown, though she would not lay eggs or develop wings. Even as a chicken, she would be a pale imitation.

I leaned down on my haunches to meet her eyes. The horn quivered as I stared down at her long painted nails and pitifully smeared mole.

"You're a virgin," I said, marveling at the words even as they formed in my mouth. "That's why you're Norma Jean and not Marilyn." I touched her forehead lightly with my thumb. "Norma Jean was innocent, and maybe—just maybe—Norma Jean was a lot more interesting."

She jumped up from the floor and ran toward one of the exits.

"How do you know?" she yelled. She tugged at the sides of her hair and tried to hide her face. The red lump bobbled as she began to cry. "You can't know that. No one knows that but King!"

I stood in front of her to shield her from the men, who were busily dressing themselves behind me.

"I can smell it," I whispered. "It's all over you."

She began screaming then, running to the door where the food cart appeared three times a day.

"Help!" she screamed. "King, please help!"

But no one answered. The men slunk away, their wool patches and manes hidden again. When she was quiet, I sat in the chair at the head of the table. No one moved to stop me. I watched as the others stared at poor Norma sobbing by the door. Some of the women tried to console her, but she pushed them away and continued to rock in the corner. The pale hand did not appear when the food arrived. The cart rolled silently inside. I nodded at the others to retrieve their plates. They slobbered at the chunks of ham as I nibbled quietly at my peanut butter and banana sandwich.

Some facts about hair:

—The average head has 100,000 hairs.

—A woman's scalp is capable of faster growth than a man's.

—If you never cut your hair, it would stop growing at approximately two and a half feet.

—The scalp generates new hair for about five years and then stops for up to three months, a kind of hair sabbatical.

—Most importantly, hair acts as a protective device. It helps the body hold in heat and acts as armor against the damaging rays of the sun.

Think of your hair as a shield.

A note arrived the next day from Crystal on stationery plastered with hound dogs. We had decided to remain in the dining room that night. The group took turns using the bathroom to assure that I was never unattended. At first several of the men tried to bar Crystal from the room, but I urged them to let her pass. With the note in my hand, I considered refusing to read it, having had more than my share of Elvis in my life. When I first glanced at it, I had an image of our parents laughing at me from somewhere in Hawaii, standing on the tarmac where Elvis had landed, Ma's bald head burned from the sun.

Dear Cass,
Don't be cruel. Please return to sender.
—King

Crystal waited for my reply while trying to assure the others that she was not there to harm me, that she was on my side.

"Like the song goes," she whispered, "it's now or never."

I lifted a black felt pen from my pocket and wrote the only response I could think of beneath King's signature:

Dear King, I wrote, *I want to leave the building.*

Crystal took the note from me and straightened my veil with her fingertips, careful not to touch the horn. I wanted her to stay with me, to tell her how sore my neck had become, how the sweat dripped down into my eyes, how I longed to see my sister again.

Return to sender, I thought, trying to remember the rest of the lyrics. *No such person . . .*

"You can count on King," Crystal said, sliding another pack of cigarettes underneath the veil. "King won't let you down."

I nodded and lit the cigarette, parting the veil so that the horn was visible to the pack. One man in the corner rubbed his fur in wide circles. Another raised his rump in the air and groaned. Several of the men had stopped pacing and stood at attention with their backs against the two-way glass, staring at me expectantly, feet apart, shoulders back.

Norma crawled across the carpet and sat at my feet. Her mole had long since faded. She picked at the crown with her fingers.

"You get more beautiful while we get worse and worse," she sighed. "On you," she said, her eyes fixed on the horn, "even *that* is becoming."

I puffed on the cigarette and offered her one. I wanted to say, "I am becoming. I am becoming," because truly, I was. Becoming what, I didn't know.

I looked down at her, at the red plumes jutting up from the top of her head. She raked her fingers through her hair, a clump falling out in her hands.

"As soon as I get out of here," she said, getting to her knees and leaning on the arm of my chair, "I'm going to change my name."

Later, after the team of doctors and orderlies had descended on us, when the bleats and screams had filled the room, I wondered if there had been some way I could have saved the others. I'd tried to charge through the door, but the volley of tranquilizer darts spinning across the room and into my arms and legs had been too much.

Sometimes, late at night when it's quiet and the air is thick with memories, I still hear them calling my name: *Cass, Cass, Cass.*

All I could see were the pairs of eyes peering at me over blue masks.

"It's time," the nurse said. She jabbed the needle into my vein, the anesthetic rushing up my arms and into my chest, down into my abdomen and running down my legs. "You've fought it long enough, but it's finally time for us to look into your head."

Spotlights shined in my eyes, the glare of floodlights spinning colors over the room. I tried to lift my head to see whose hands gripped my thighs, whose fingers snaked through my hair and over the base of the horn. Straps scraped my ankles, belt buckles dug into my skin. The sounds of zipping, unzipping, as fingers moved from the base of the horn and up to the tip, down and around and up again, moving faster. I heard stifled moans, the sharp cries of desire.

Someone screamed the opening line to "Heartbreak Hotel."

When I looked up, straining to see past the horn and behind me, I saw Anderson smiling down with his *chai* hanging above my head, his blond curls twisted into a golden puff. The chain around his neck sparkled in the light as he squeezed the sides of my head so tightly I thought my skull would collapse.

"Such a beauty," he said. The tip of his scalpel gleamed. "Such a shame."

If only I'd cooperated, he told me in a whisper. If only I'd eaten the ham I'd been given. If only I'd quietly smoked Camels, filled out the forms, and hadn't asked so many questions. Someone as beautiful as I was, he said, had an obligation to be watched. It was part of the territory, he laughed in my ear.

I felt Vance beside him even before I looked up to find him standing in the corner with the scalpel in his hand. He was dressed in a white jumpsuit with a red, white, and blue eagle in dotted spangles across his chest. Behind him, a cape swished. His hips swiveled as he moved across the room.

Anderson lifted the *chai* to his lips and kissed it, then slapped Vance on the back.

"Keratin," he said to Vance. "Just the thing you've been waiting for."

Vance stepped forward and held the blade over my head.

"Did you think I would let you go, Cass?" he panted. "Did you think I would let this slip out of my hands?"

He moved to touch the horn with his fingertips, but I jerked my head away and felt the horn thumping.

"For Christ's sake, Vance," I said. I struggled to pull myself free of the restraints, daring them to come closer. The horn throbbed as I watched the two of them leaning down toward me. Vance had pathetically glued fake hair to the sides of his face in the famous lamb chop sideburns.

"You can't even grow back a goddamned toenail, you *shmuck*," I said.

He set the scalpel down on the table beside him and moved toward me.

"I'm not going to hurt you, Cass," he said, gold rings splayed across his fingers, a diamond T.C.B. pendant on his chest. "I would never hurt you. I just want to touch it," he breathed. "What you've got on your head does not make you any different from other women."

He laughed then and grabbed the horn with both hands before I could stop him.

"Admit it," he said. "Elvis makes you horny."

He jumped on top of me. The scalpel fell to the floor. A sharp clang reverberated through the room. I thrashed beneath him, jabbing at his chest with my head, over and over again, struggling to slam my head through his rib cage, to stun him into submission. He wouldn't let go, both hands gripping the horn, his body flailing like an epileptic, my body shot through with electricity.

The horn surged as he convulsed above me. His fingers still wrapped around the horn, as if he would tear it off with his bare hands, as if he would yank it from my head if he could, pull out my brain along with it, leave me a gurgling mass of blood, bone, and drool.

I thought I was free when he rolled off me and sat gasping on the floor. I wriggled to free myself, and just as I'd finally unpinned my right arm, he appeared at my side again, the scalpel just inches from the horn.

"Go ahead," I snorted. "Do it."

I heard Anderson laughing.

"Yes," he said, "do it."

Vance got to his knees and straddled me, the bones of his buttocks weighing down my rib cage. He looked down at me, a million regrown toenails flashing in his eyes, and brought the blade down with both hands.

The tip of the scalpel scraped the edge of the horn. I closed my eyes and waited. Suddenly, I felt a strange sense of freedom as I heard the thud of bodies being thrown against the wall. A terrible crash echoed through the room, then the pounding of feet and frothy snarls. My breath was ragged and fierce, burning my lungs.

The air grew thick, and above my head, the light suffused with red, white, and blue streams of color. As the straps fell away, I saw nothing but the blur of black hair ahead of me. I ran toward the hair, my feet pounding the tile floor. I followed for as long as I could, down a winding hallway, up flights of stairs, until finally a sheen of light appeared before us, and we were off. The doors flung open. The air turned a blinding white.

"King," I whispered, stumbling, "is it really you?"

The voice was breathy, but I heard my name whispered, and then the words, "Sattnin, oh, Sattnin."

He disappeared down a dark hallway, a white cape swirling in the air. I walked to the door he'd led me to and opened it. The rush of night air cooled my arms as I ran toward the gates in the distance.

PART V

An image is one thing,
and a human being is another.
It's very hard
to live up to an image.

—ELVIS PRESLEY

SEVENTEEN

Crystal's hair set me free.

I'd made it to the end of an open field but couldn't get past the double-bolted gates marked "High Voltage." Without the veil, I knew how dangerous the horn might become, especially if I were spotted on the street.

Standing in front of that gate and terrified to touch it for fear of being shocked—and of what lay beyond it—I suddenly knew how trapped Lena felt. And I knew she couldn't spend the rest of her life feeling that way.

Just as I was about to turn back to look for another exit, Crystal appeared with the white cape in her hands.

"You're going to need this," she said, motioning for me to turn around as she snapped it around my shoulders.

I reached up to cover the horn with my hands, but she pulled them gently to my sides.

"Here," she said, hooking my fingers in the ends of the extensions I'd spent so many hours attaching. "You'll need these more than I will."

Together we pulled the extensions loose, yanking brittle pieces of her own hair with them. I tried to protest as I saw how badly damaged her hair would be, but she urged me on until I'd unraveled several feet of the dark hair. As I bent down to scoop it up, she motioned for me to sit on the ground and reached out toward the horn.

Before I could say anything, she wrapped the strands around the horn, then pulled bobby pins from her coat pockets to fasten them to the hair on my head. She stepped away and helped me to my feet.

"What are you doing?" I asked.

She shushed me and placed her hands on my shoulders to look at my reflection in the metal edge of the gate.

She'd given me a pompadour.

I laughed suddenly, louder than I'd laughed in months, and she laughed, too, the two of us caught in a burst of giggles that seemed to never want to stop.

"You know," she said, reaching toward the gate and pushing several buttons to unlock it, "the first time I saw you, I knew you had a lot of Elvis in you."

I smiled.

"Thank you, Crystal," I said, reaching forward to hug her.

I breathed in the leather smell of the cape as she hugged me tightly against her.

"Thankyouverymuch," I whispered.

She waved to me as I walked away. I turned once to look back at her. The shorn strands of her hair shifted in the wind as the doors opened, and I headed out into the darkness of the night.

Lena and I knew our parents were having sex whenever we heard the thundering sounds of the "Theme from *2001: A Space Odyssey,*" Elvis's famed intro—what I later learned was also known as "Thus Spake Zarathustra"—coming from their room. For years Lena would cover her ears whenever she heard the slow blare of horns and heavy kettle drums because she couldn't block out the image of our parents locked and humping together.

There are things a kid shouldn't know.

It took me nearly five hours to walk back to Lena's house.

On the road outside the hospital I tried to stay out of the streetlights. Then, as dawn approached, I stopped in front of a church to catch my breath. I wondered if I should go inside, get down on my knees and pray.

"Monday, Monday," I sang. Some things you just can't escape.

I sat down on the front steps and watched a group of young women on the other side of the street smoking cigarettes and laughing. One of the women pointed at me and nudged her friend.

"Hey, look at that!" she called, waving at me. "Hey, Elvis!"

I ducked my head, pulled the cape up over my shoulders and started to run down the street.

"Elvis has left the planet," I called back. "Leave Elvis alone."

They started to chase me, shouting, "Elvis, Elvis!" But they must have given up, because when I turned back, I heard only faint voices.

Later, as I approached the house, I thought I saw Norma, Janis, and some of the men pacing along a nearby sidewalk. They stopped and lit cigarettes under cupped hands. In the darkness, their maladies disappeared. They could have been anyone standing there smoking together, any group of old friends, or even a pack of strangers who had happened upon each other. They appeared neither beautiful, ugly, or terribly plain.

I knew it couldn't have been them, not really, but imagining the sounds of their feet scraping the pavement brought me an odd sense of comfort. When I got closer to Lena's house, I turned back to wave good-bye to them, to wish them well, but they were gone.

The house came into view as I turned the corner. On the porch Lena's begonias and geraniums bloomed. Droplets clung to the leaves, as if they'd been freshly watered, but there was no sign of Ernie's mail truck. The house was dark and eerily quiet, and as I ran up the porch steps, I wondered how she'd managed alone all these nights without me.

I reached into the pocket of my jeans for my key, digging with my fingers, but all I found were some matches, frayed and bent. I didn't want to alarm Lena by waking her out of a dream—a frequent trigger for a panic attack—but I had no other way to get in.

With my knuckles I tapped lightly at the door, softly at first, and then louder when I got no response. I banged harder, even though I was sure I would wake up the neighbors—the doorbell had long since broken, and why hadn't we fixed it? All the business with my head had left me disoriented, and in my haste to get to the hospital, I'd never considered how I might get back inside.

"Lena!" I called, "Lena!" and when she didn't answer, I imagined her lying on her bed with a bottle of Xanax in her hand and too many squashed dreams of our parents returning.

I rammed my head against the door and shouted her name. Over and over I charged, head first, the horn banging against the door, threatening to burst it down. I hit the door head-on, the horn crunching with the force.

On the fourth try, the lights went on, and I charged the door one last time. A wave of pain shot through my head. I swayed, leaned against the doorjamb to steady myself. As I heard Lena shuffling toward the door, the horn cracked at the base and fell at my feet right there on the porch, right into the pile of Crystal's hair extensions.

I picked it up and held the horn in my hands, untangling it from the mass of hair. It felt brittle, flakes of skin falling onto the porch floor as I moved my fingers over it. The air surged in my lungs. As quickly as I could, I shoved the horn and the hair under the cape as Lena flung open the door.

"Cass!" she cried, reaching for me. "Cass, where the hell have you been?"

We held each other for a long time as I thought of how to possibly explain everything that had happened to me—how I'd been trapped by a crazy *goy* doctor, how I'd lived in a zoo-like place named Castlewood where everyone had been burdened with the names of famous dead people. About Vance the toe-hacker who had tried to have his way with my head. About my horn, the power I'd wielded just by virtue of the growth on my head.

About the freedom I felt.

"I've been worried sick," she said, and I nodded, feeling the cat's tail swish between my legs.

We looked down at her bare toes with the missing toenail. They looked so pretty to me in the moonlight, prettier than any feet I'd ever seen. Lena looked up at me then.

"You have such pretty feet," I said. She reached for both of my hands to pull me inside. "Yeah," she said, smiling, "I guess I still do."

Anyone who has ever been agoraphobic—or has experienced the sensation of growing and then losing a six-inch horn on her head—knows that a return to normalcy is not easy. You don't just wake up to find you can go outside and run barefoot in the grass or that you can walk by a mirror without checking to see what has become of your head.

Some people spend their whole lives without ever think-ing about what goes on in their heads.

I haven't been one of those people.

I kept the horn wrapped in tissue paper and hid it under the twin bed at Lena's house. When she asked how the procedure had gone and why I'd never called, I gave her cryptic answers. The doctors had been kind to me, the operation painless. After the anesthesia I'd been groggy, and it had taken time for the bandages to come off.

"The important thing is that it's over," I told her.

She lit a cigarette and logged on for her session with the internet shrink.

"Well, you look as beautiful as you ever have," she said.

I smiled and read over her shoulder as her shrink spelled out the lyrics to yet another Elvis song.

"Maybe someday," I said, "I'll tell you the whole story."

She turned around to face me. With the light behind her and her face framed by the glow of the computer screen, she gave me a sad smile and snapped at the rubber band on her wrist.

"I could use another story," she said.

Griz jumped in my lap and settled into a ball. Her heat had passed, and she no longer seemed concerned with sniffing at my head.

"Not that kind of story," I said. "I think there have been enough of those, don't you?"

She shrugged and turned back to the computer screen.

In the bathroom, I pulled my hair away from my face and stared at the point on my forehead where the horn had grown. Pieces of dry skin still clung there. A reddish spot still emanated heat. When we went to bed later that night, I didn't wash my face or apply moisturizer or do any of the nightly rituals I'd become accustomed to. I just laid my head on the pillow and let my arm dangle off the side of the bed. A few times I turned on my side to reach under the bed for the horn, but it seemed to elude me, lurking just out of reach.

I left the house in the middle of the night to meet Ernie. He drove me out toward the hospital, where I found my car outside the gates, a parking ticket on my windshield. From the distance I tried to make out the name, Castlewood, but it was too dark to see. Ernie looked tired, ragged, and I couldn't help but feel a stab of pity for him for having to do so much for us, to not only drive me back to the hospital but to take care of Lena in my absence, watering her plants and checking on her nightly. Lena told me that Ernie had slept on the porch by the mail slot several nights until she'd finally pleaded with him to go home.

Before I got into my car, he stopped me and riffled through his mail bag.

"I meant to tell you that I did my best to trace that letter," he said, fumbling through a stack of papers. "The one with no return address."

He reached into his bag and produced the tattered envelope. I turned on the headlights to get a better look. The postmark had faded even more.

"I never believed in untraceable mail before," he said, "but we tried everywhere. Graceland, inner-city Memphis, even Tupelo, Mississippi. I thought maybe they'd go back to where Elvis was born."

He smiled sadly and tapped at his mailbag with his fingertips.

"I tried my best, Cass," he said. "I hope you can believe me. I really did try."

As we stood there by my car for what seemed like minutes, I thought of blurting, "I've had a horn on my head, Ernie," but now that it was gone, who would believe me?

I assured him that I knew how hard he'd tried and thanked him for all he'd done for us. Although some people might think it would be helpful to know where my parents are after all these years, I am not one of those people.

"Let's not mention the letter," I said, patting his mailbag. "Unless Lena asks what happened to it. Too much excitement is no good for her. At least that's what all the shrinks say."

I got into the car and started the engine. Ernie nodded and handed me the envelope and a red pen. Across the top, I wrote, *Return to Sender. No Such Person. No Such Zone.*

I felt hot tears welling up in my eyes.

"Cass," he said, "is everything all right? Is everything all right with your head?"

I plucked the parking ticket off the windshield, got in, and rolled down the window.

"Sure, Ernie," I said, "everything's fine. Everything's going to be fine now."

I waved as I pulled away and turned the corner. Halfway back to my house, I stopped at the side of the road. Under one of the streetlights, I pressed my head against the steering wheel and cried for my parents. Not just because they'd left us so long ago, and not just because they had been chasing a dream that didn't exist, a dream that had never existed, but because, until that moment, I hadn't understood.

On the last day of Elvis's life, he refused to eat. Some say the prescription drugs had made him lose his appetite, all those packets of pills to help him sleep, wake up, carry on with the business of being Elvis Presley. His cook had wanted to make him his usual breakfast, but that day, he wanted only water.

"All I want," he said, "is some cold water."

At around 2 p.m., he slipped into the bathroom to read, and he never came out.

He fell down and cracked his head, and all the King's men couldn't put him back together again.

You have to admit: it's a sad, sad story.

EIGHTEEN

I've heard all the jokes.

What do you call a woman with no forehead and a cap pulled over her eyes?

Horny.

What's the difference between a woman with a horn and a man with a small penis?

About six inches.

What do you call a woman with a six-inch horn on her head and nothing else?

My kind of gal.

Not one of them has made me laugh.

I went to Regal's to collect my last paycheck without bothering to check my reflection or even smear gloss on my lips. I wore my hair pulled back in a ponytail, used no gel, no spritz to create shine and fullness, no foundation to conceal the rawness where the horn had erupted. Several of the clients stared at me as I made my way to my station. I stared back as long strands of highlighted hair were being attached to hide their shortcomings and to maintain the illusion that they'd just come in from the sun.

I wanted to tell them that restoring their hair would not make up for what they'd lost. We can make them look good when we're finished, but we can never fix their problems. We can never change the way they feel or who they are. We can never get inside.

Maureen wept openly as I collected the brushes, special combs, clips, and adhesives I'd used so well.

"There's nothing I can do to convince you to stay?" she asked, wiping her eyes with a tissue I handed her. "You don't even need to cover that spot on your head if you don't want to," she said. "You're beautiful even without makeup."

Selena gave me three different kinds of peppermint conditioner and an article on toenail growth she'd read in a professional journal.

"For your sister and her toenail problem," she said. "It looks like there may be hope, *mammele.*" She opened the journal to a page she'd earmarked. "They think that this keratin is the key to growing back dead toenails," she said. "But the rhinoceros is an endangered species, so they can't use the horn. They're trying to look elsewhere, but so far no luck."

She pressed the journal in my hands and kissed my cheek. She had no idea what she was saying, and I decided not to hold it against her.

"It might give your sister something to look forward to," she said. "Finding a cure for her problem."

I thanked her and slid the journal into my bag. Selena took my hand in hers and stared at the red spot on my head.

"Don't you worry," she said, "it will go away." She pressed her lips to the spot on my forehead and kissed it. I held my breath and swallowed back the tears.

"These hair products, this Rogaine, these additions," she whispered. "What is it we're selling? None of it is real. Telling them that fixing their hair can change their lives is nothing but *bobe-mayse.*"

Joan was waiting for me in the back parking lot with a joint in her hand. If I were going to leave her alone at Regal's with all those bald women, she said, the least I could do was get high with her one last time.

"Come on," she said. "Let's smoke this before Cousin It comes in."

I shoved the box into the back seat and felt the blood rush to my head. She handed me the joint, and I took a quick hit before handing it back to her, blowing out the smoke before it reached my lungs.

"Her name's Crystal," I said. "And she knows what we call her."

Joan shrugged and took another long drag.

"Well, that was bound to happen," she said. "The main thing is, you took care of your head."

I slid the combs and brushes into the large black bag I'd been carrying.

"You didn't let that toe-hacker get at it, did you?" she asked, narrowing her eyes at me.

I smiled and reached over to squeeze her shoulder.

"No," I said. "I never did."

Later I asked Lena to play a game of "Where Are They Now?" She was sitting in the living room watching the Home Shopping Network but snapped off the remote immediately at the suggestion of the game. In the past Lena had imagined them in Hawaii covered in so many leis they could barely breathe. I'd conjured up images of the two of them dancing outside the gates of Graceland, Our Father's hand on Ma's waist as they did the Lindy over and over again. Sometimes we pictured them in Vegas among the glitz and the showgirls, Our Father on stage in a sparkling jumpsuit, beaming out at Ma in the front row.

"o.k.," she said, reaching for her pack of cigarettes. She lit one and eyed me nervously. "Where do you want to pretend they are?"

I sat in the recliner across from her with Griz in my lap, her rump in the air as I stroked her back. The envelope was still folded neatly in the pocket of my jeans. I could have easily handed it over to her and said, "Ernie couldn't find them. And neither will we."

But I knew that would do neither of us any good. I was tired of this game, of all the illusions we'd been living with— all the ways I'd played a part in this fantasy. I took a deep breath, the space in my forehead still aching, and blurted out the first thing that came to mind.

"Let's pretend they're dead," I said.

For a long time she said nothing, just smoked the cigarette all the way down to the filter and sat staring at the blank television screen. Griz's tail twitched back and forth as if she were ready to pounce. I didn't dare move as Lena's breath grew quicker and more shallow, her chest and arms covered in pink spots like strawberry marks.

"Dead?" she breathed. "Really dead?"

I nodded and waited for her to start screaming. I reached up to cover my ears.

But then she just stubbed out the cigarette and looked at me. A thick cloud of smoke hovered in the air between us.

"o.k.," she said finally. "o.k."

That night I dug out all the things they'd left behind and laid them in a box: the frayed pages of the tell-all book that had been Elvis's undoing, the ticket to the concert they were to attend a week after his death, the magazines and newspaper clippings yellowed with age.

"A Lonely Life Ends on Elvis Presley Boulevard" read one of the headlines.

I covered the headline with a picture of Elvis in his youth with a pompadour, lip curled, eyes glinting even in the black-and-white print. It was unfair for anyone to live up to that kind of beauty, I thought, carrying the box into the bedroom. And even when he was no longer beautiful, when he seemed to no longer care, the world had seen the glimmer of what he'd once been. I wondered if he'd ever truly realized who he was, what it meant to be Elvis, if that was the one thing he'd never been able to understand. I wondered if he ever realized that he was more than just his beauty. In all his searching, I wondered if he'd ever found out why he and he alone had been Elvis Presley, and why, despite all the imitators, there would never be another.

When I finished packing the box, I got down on my hands and knees and reached under the bed for the horn. I unwrapped it from the tissue paper and held it in my hands, letting my fingers feel the rough skin that surrounded it like calluses, the flesh hard as bone. Pieces of it had already begun to peel away, flakes of skin floating down over the clippings.

I was about to lay it on top of the other pieces of Elvis memorabilia when Lena stepped forward and blew cigarette smoke over the top of the box. She threw the pieces of laminated dental floss and toenail clippings in and looked up at me.

"Are you going to be all right without it?" she asked.

I dropped what was left of the horn into the box and stared down at it, gray and lifeless. The space on my head throbbed and then relaxed, my whole head filling with warmth.

"Yeah," I said, turning toward her. "Are you?"

She nodded, flicked ashes into the box, and then let several Xanax fall from her hand and land on Elvis's face. We both laughed. I put my arm around her shoulder and squeezed. Without a word she dumped the contents of the ashtray into the box. Before I sealed it with duct tape, I covered everything with the white cape Crystal had given me and then shoved the hair on top.

The tape made a scraping sound as I secured the last piece. I closed my eyes and ran my fingertips over the box one last time. Lena stepped toward me and blew a kiss at the top of the box, taking the tape from my hands and dropping it on the floor. We each took a deep breath, grabbed each other's hands, and spun around and around, faster and faster, until we both let go and stood there, watching the room move in and out of focus.

I wish I could say that after we buried the contents of our parent's lives and the horn that had sprouted from my head had just as suddenly broken off, leaving behind only sore spots and memories, that Lena had left the house. I wish I could tell you that she'd stood in the doorway as Ernie and I dug the hole and covered the box in mounds of dirt, that she'd stepped off the back porch and onto the grass, feeling the earth under her toes. I wish I could tell you that after Ellen Graham, who had lost her father to Sinatra, had arrived for a *shiva* call with a basket of fruit, that Lena had gotten up and ran straight out the door.

But she'd only stood at the window smoking and watching, her face pressed against the glass as Ernie held his mail hat over his heart, and I'd said the only Hebrew prayer I knew.

I wish I could tell you that Crystal had come to sing a rousing version of "Monday, Monday," and that Ernie, Joan, and I had harmonized to "Blue Eyes Crying in the Rain," the last song Elvis had ever sung on this earth.

I wish I could say that afterwards we'd all eaten ham sandwiches on dry bread and that I no longer feared choking.

Or I wish I could tell you I'd become a Jew.

I wish I could tell you that I'd buried the horn and that was where the story ends.

There are some things I keep to myself.

Like hair replacement, it's a kind of self-preservation.

I could tell you that the toe-hacker lived, that Joan and I still smoked joints together, that I went on to a stunning career in celebrity hair replacement, that I once worked on the hair of a woman who looked remarkably like Ma.

I could tell you that Lena never gave up trying to leave the house, that I'd stood behind her as she wrapped her hand around the doorknob, but was never able to open the door more than a crack, enough to let in just a little bit of light.

I could tell you all these things, but I won't.

I can tell you this:

I think about how it felt to have a horn on my head, even though I try not to think about it unless I'm asked.

Sometimes I think about the things that bring me comfort: Lena and I spinning in our childhood bedroom, Selena's lips pressed to my forehead, the dry taste of *matzoh* on my tongue, Joan and I quietly sipping lattes in my kitchen, the kindness of Ernie's smile.

And sometimes I even think about Elvis.

ACKNOWLEDGMENTS

Deepest thanks go to Esther Sung for her belief in me and in this book, and to my editor and publisher, Allan Kornblum, whose sharp vision and insights raise the bar every time; to the staff of Coffee House Press, for their commitment and dedication; to all of the people who gave me Elvis memorabilia as lucky charms, especially Sarah Fasso, for the life-size cardboard Elvis that stood guard every day; to the writers of the many books for information on Elvis, among them Priscilla Presley, *Elvis and Me;* June Juanico, *Elvis in the Twilight of Memory;* Greil Marcus, *Dead Elvis;* Peter H. Brown and Pat H. Broeske, *Down at the End of Lonely Street;* Frank Coffey, *The Complete Idiot's Guide to Elvis;* with particular appreciation for the wonderful books by Peter Guralnick, *Last Train to Memphis* and *Careless Love;* to the MacDowell Colony and the Virginia Center for the Creative Arts for their support, and above all, the time; love and thanks also to Cody Collett for candles, courage, and inspiration, always; Katherine Oxnard for her ebullient spirit and open heart; Alison McGhee for her friendship, words, and wisdom; and Judith Dupré for blessing the last eighty pages and so much more; and to my parents, hilarious storytellers, with love to my mother, for giving me life, love, and Elvis, and for sharing that first trip to Graceland, and to my father, for his courage, his strength, his hair, and his appreciation for my mind; to Eugene Ionesco, for *Rhinoceros,* which changed everything; and finally, to my husband, Michael, for the love, laughter, and understanding that make it all not only possible but worthwhile.

FUNDER ACKNOWLEDGMENT

Coffee House Press is an independent nonprofit literary publisher. Our books are made possible through the generous support of grants and gifts from many foundations, corporate giving programs, individuals, and through state and federal support. This book received special project support from the National Endowment for the Arts, a federal agency. Coffee House Press receives general operating support from the Minnesota State Arts Board, through an appropriation by the Minnesota State Legislature and from the National Endowment for the Arts, a federal agency. Coffee House receives major funding from the McKnight Foundation, and from Target. Coffee House also receives significant support from an anonymous donor; the Buuck Family Foundation; the Bush Foundation; the Patrick and Aimee Butler Family Foundation; Consortium Book Sales and Distribution; the Foundation for Contemporary Performance Arts; Stephen and Isabel Keating; the Lerner Family Foundation; the Outagamie Foundation; the Pacific Foundation; the law firm of Schwegman, Lundberg, Woessner & Kluth, P.A.; the James R. Thorpe Foundation; West Group; the Woessner Freeman Family Foundation; and many other generous individual donors.

This activity is made possible in part by a grant from the Minnesota State Arts Board, through an appropriation by the Minnesota State Legislature and a grant from the National Endowment for the Arts.

MINNESOTA
STATE ARTS BOARD

NATIONAL
ENDOWMENT
FOR THE ARTS

To you and our many readers across the country, we send our thanks for your continuing support.

Good books are brewing at coffeehousepress.org